The Treasure

....

A Fun Romp Through the
Amazon with Love, Adventure and
Headhunters

Richard E. LaMotte

Publisher: Cloud Dancer Productions

Contents

Chapter 1

I t was a strange night, dark and foreboding. The monsoon had raged for hours. Giant clouds crawled across the sky, blotted out the moon and stars, and unleashed a roaring downpour that savaged the thick green jungle of the upper Amazon. The inky blackness was rent by bursts of jagged lightning and the crackling tear of thunder; and the local Indians hid, thinking the Gods were angry.

Jim Ives, a middle-aged Irishman, suddenly woke to something—what was it—the buffeting wind that whistled through the bamboo walls of his small shack—the thumping tattoo of rain beating against the thatch roof? He listened quietly, rubbing his stubbled chin, trying to clear the hangover that still had him groggy.

His battered hut squatted at the edge of a small tributary where he slept on a dirty cot under a stained mosquito net—now something had awakened him, and he reached for his pistol as he swung his feet to the floor, and questioned with a raspy growl, "Who's there? *Quien es?*"

A pang of fear shot thru him. In the open doorway, he saw a man-sized shadow, and he realized he wasn't alone. A sudden flash of lightning illuminated the figure in relief. Barely discernible in the back light, a wild looking little man, draped in an old Indian blanket, slouched in the opening.

Jim froze and took aim, but the doorway, illuminated again by lightning, was empty—whoever had been there was gone, and a long crackle of rolling thunder underscored the strange encounter.

Jim limped to the door. He looked out through the sheeting water into his dark wet surroundings—and saw faintly a man's muddy tracks being washed away by the downpour. Soon they were gone. Only the storm remained. He leaned against the door frame, hovering at the edge of disbelief. Had he been dreaming? What woke him? He realized he had awakened, not because of some noise, but because of some *feeling*. Some uneasiness had dragged him back into a fearful consciousness.

A slight movement caught his eye—a dirty, string-bound letter was stuck to the doorpost by a small knife. Jim took the letter and looked again for any sign of the mysterious messenger.

"What the hell?" he mumbled, taking the soiled envelope in his hands. The address, written in a feverish scrawl, suddenly illuminated by a close electric flash, read: "To Tom Jackman, World Rubber Company, New York, New York, U.S.A." Jim winced at the close peel of thunder.

• • • • • • • • • • •

Upstate New York. A stately beaux arts mansion rested behind a tree-lined driveway. Known locally as The Gardens, its beautifully manicured grounds of trees, fountains, hedges, and rose-beds sparkled in the clear morning sunlight.

The voice of an angry woman disturbed the tranquility. "Tom Jackman! He's a cheater and you know it!"

Linda Dawson stalked the drawing room like a caged tigress. At twenty-five, the former showgirl was dancer trim and beautiful. As she paced, her tousled blond hair bounced around her rounded, sensuous features. One hand clutched her Japanese kimono closed, while the other waved the front section of a newspaper. She stopped and faced the man seated in a large Chippendale wing chair—Tom Jackman, her lawyer. At thirty-five, he was handsome, well-tailored, and oozed a controlled and superior manner.

"Linda, please calm down." He tried to reassure her with a measured tone, "We don't know what happened, not really." He used his most dashing smile.

But Linda wasn't a bit calm. "Maybe you don't know what happened, but I do. This is some little trick of Truman's." She stabbed the front page with her finger, letting her kimono fall slightly open while she brushed loose hair from her forehead.

The revealed skin between her breasts drew Tom's momentary attention. "Now, Linda...." he cautioned, while watching her athletic body move under the silk material.

"Don't you 'now, Linda' me," she said in a frustrated tone.

"I mean we just have to wait—"

"Wait? That's great advice from you—you're a lawyer and you're paid by the hour." She shook the paper at him.

Tom smiled a little condescendingly, leaned back in his chair, templed his hands and crossed his legs. She was on a tear and there was no stopping her, so why escalate her mood?

Linda, exhausted, groaned with disappointment as she sank into a chair across from him. Panic drove thoughts through her mind. She was about to lose everything, and no one seemed to care.

Tom waited a slow minute, watching Linda's face contort through a series of emotions, finally settling into hopelessness. He leaned forward with the superior demeanor of an adult about to correct a dim-witted child.

"All I mean—and Linda, you'd do well to try and follow this," he said using his practiced sincere tone, "is that, as your family's personal attorney, I'm in a better position to, shall we say, more correctly assess the relative legal positions of you and the company which Truman, your husband, owns."

"Cheating, two-timing, lying husband in hiding."

"Hastiness is ill-advised."

"Hastiness, my ass, Tom! All this is a lot of legal mumbo jumbo."

"What do you mean?"

Linda stood again and walked to the window, biting her thumb nail, trying to think. Tom watched the kimono ripple over her undulating body, the print suggesting red and yellow carp swimming through lily pads.

She suddenly turned back. "What do I mean? Look, I know what people say about us—that because he picked me out of a chorus line, I'm a little gold-digger who married Truman for his money—that I seduced some poor old innocent rich guy in his second childhood—that I could never love a man over twice my age, hell, three times. And that I have no real right to anything of his—not his name, or his money, or his business."

She paused again, looking to Tom for some encouraging response.

He maintained an uncomfortable silence.

She continued, a little more dispirited. "Maybe a little of that is true, but when I met him, he wasn't old. Truman was elegant. He'd been everywhere and done everything. He told me how special I was. How he was ready to settle down and have a family—how he was happy for the first time in his life—my God, Tom, I was so thrilled...flattered. Maybe I played at being Cinderella, but he knew what he was doing. Besides, I tried to love him...I did love him...." She softened at a memory...and sniffed. "God, I am stupid." She turned back to the window, trying to hide her tears.

Tom came up behind her, attracted as much by her vulnerability as her voluptuousness. He let his hands gently take ahold of her arms, felt her soft skin beneath his fingers, and moved closer, smelling her freshly washed hair. "Yes, I remember. No one had ever seen Truman happier—what happened?" His voice sounded unexpectedly horse.

She twisted away. "He got tired of me. I wasn't his intellectual equal, maybe I was too human, too much the farm girl and not enough showgirl. I complained about his business too...."

"What do you mean by that?" Her comment, related to World Rubber company business, reminded Tom of his moneyed interests and rekindled his legal attention.

"He could be a monster," she went on, "Lie, cheat, steal—anything for money. We would argue about it sometimes, then one day he left for his place in the jungle and never came back—now the board of directors is trying to find a way to get the marriage annulled and throw me overboard without a cent."

Tom silently mulled over her revelation. Truman could be everything she said—true, so could almost every wealthy businessman, to one degree or another. But her concern about her future and her inside knowledge of Truman's business practices might offer some sort of leverage with the company. In any event, the stakes were now a bit greater, several millions actually. If he played his cards right, he might profit no matter whose interests prevailed. He had to gain some time and be the voice of reason while he made a deeper assessment of the struggle between the interests involved. After all, in confusion there was always opportunity.

"They're not throwing you out," he started, "all they're saying is that, in Truman's extended absence, they're assuming emergency powers."

"Yes," Linda's voice rose, imploring his understanding, "and freezing me with the rest of his assets. Don't you get it? I don't share his bank account. He gave me an allowance to buy things with—that's it!" He could see her brows knit. "I've been able to save a little money, but another few weeks and I'll be back doing two shows a day at the Roxy for drunks wearing overcoats, while Truman hides in the jungle with his bank book, laughing at me."

She collapsed into the plush wing chair in frustration, her hands running through her hair. Her large eyes, luminous with tears, looked up to Tom, pleading for an answer.

Tom considered for a moment. *God, she's beautiful,* he thought, quickly imagining what she would look like.... He resisted his baser instincts.

"Whatever's happened, this is about more than just you and Truman." He offered, "let me see what I can do."

Tom turned away and tried to formulate some kind of plan. "I'll meet with the board, find out what I can, and we'll meet later," he turned back, smiling.

"There's no time." She spat, suddenly angry all over again. She pushed herself up out of the chair. "I have to go to New York and face them myself!"

"What? Linda, you can't do that," Tom stammered, watching her jaw muscles flex, knowing his plans could be ruined before he would have a chance to lay any advantageous groundwork.

Linda went on, adamantly, "I have to find a way to turn the tables on them...I have to. If Truman had been man enough to talk to me, I would have done anything to make him happy—but now? Don't you see, I can't let him just throw my life away...I've been poor, it sucks. I'm not going to be poor again, not without a fight."

Tom said nothing. He knew that dealing with head-strong people was like fishing—reel them in, and then let them loose a little to play themselves out, to let them tire themselves before they became more resistive. From his point of view, that was the one thing wrong with Linda. She was determined to have her own way, sometimes acting capriciously against his advice.

Perhaps that was the trouble with all modern women, he thought, *too headstrong.*

Linda looked down at the newspaper in her hand. Under the continuing news of the 1934 depression, the headline read: "TRUMAN DAWSON, RUBBER TYCOON, MISSING IN THE AMAZON JUNGLE—PRESUMED DEAD". Below was a map of South America.

Oh, Truman, where are you? She asked herself as she raised her fist to her mouth and bit her thumbnail.

Chapter 2

Iquitos was a small jungle town, rotting in the humidity of the upper Amazon. It lay at the convergence of two broad, muddy rivers and was a study in contradictions. Aside from a few regular buildings, it was laced with canals lined with vendor stalls, and native dwellings hovering above the water on stilts, a motley collection of wood, adobe, tin and bamboo, half overgrown by a voracious jungle trying to reclaim it. Yet close by, a few luxurious mansions owned largely by absentee rubber barons rested behind iron gates.

· · · · ● · ● · · ·

Jim Ives landed his canoe along a tree shaded quay and made his way through the exotic sights and sounds of the tropical marketplace. He limped noticeably. His right leg was stiff at the knee, the legacy of a German artillery shell. He meandered through the warren of stalls and cathouses until he came to the old Spanish colonial building with a sign above the doors that read, WORLD RUBBER COMPANY.

Jim paused for a moment in front of the building as he gave the soiled envelope in his hand a last thought...then pushed his way through the front door.

He crossed the tiled floor, under adobe arches splotched with mold, past desks where tired men in rumpled suits labored over stacks of paper under squeaky ceiling fans, and finally entered an office marked: MANAGER.

The office was small and smelled of rot and cigar smoke. A little owlish man sat across the desk from Jim. Mister Johnson looked up from what he was reading with his small beady eyes and asked, "Whadda ya want, Jim?"

Jim stammered, "I got something worth...something." He licked his lips, unprepared for any real negotiation, or Johnson's withering gaze.

Johnson continued to watch Jim as he sat back, a half-smoked cigar in his mouth, and ran his thumbs under his striped suspenders. "Well, spit it out kiddo, I ain't no mind reader."

Jim handed over the letter slowly. "It's to Tom Jackman. Important I'll bet...worth, who knows how much?"

"It's mail, Jim. You can't charge to deliver the mail."

Jim snatched the letter back.

"You're right, you're right. Maybe I'll just write a little missive and send it on meself and see if Mister Jackman here would help an old soldier with a little reward."

Johnson regarded Jim and blinked. "Old bandit's more like it."

Moments later, Jim emerged from the office, stuffing a small wad of local bills into his shirt pocket. He whistled "The Irish Washerwoman" as he continued down the street. His limp became a skip as he quickened his pace toward the sound of raucous laughter.

· · · ● · ● ● · ·

The Sampan Saloon was a typical river front dive. Jim passed a dozen local soldiers who lounged around the dock in front. A look of pleasant expectation lit Jim's face as he entered through the broken shuttered doors to the driving sound of impromptu Samba music.

The smell of stale beer, sweat, and urine-soaked linoleum floors rushed to meet Jim as he pushed his way past potted palms, vicious looking river-rats, and seedy hookers, to the bar, where another American was having a drink with a local captain of the river police and a dark-eyed woman whose best years were waning fast.

"Laddie!" he yelled, as he slapped the other American on the back.

Sam Black turned from the bar, his face breaking into a friendly, handsome smile; all tan skin stretched over tight muscles. He had the look of a bush hunter and guide, brimming with confidence, life, and swagger under a three-day growth of beard.

"Jimmy boy!" he answered, smiling, pushing his salty campaign hat jauntily back on his head.

They all shook hands and exchanged grins, including Luis Castillo, the river police captain.

Sam ordered another bottle with a whistle and a nod. "What are you doing down here?"

"Just running some errands, boyo. Yourself?"

"Aww, Captain Castillo hired me to take him upriver."

"La Merced?"

"Nah, the other way, up past your place." The bottle came, and Sam poured a round.

"Why? I thought all the trouble was more north, along the plantation route."

Sam and Castillo shared a look but said nothing.

"I get it, military secret, huh?

"Discretion is the better part of valor, *amigo*," said Castillo, looking around. "Besides, one never knows who's listening in this place."

They threw down their drinks as a soldier entered and saluted Castillo. "*Estamos listos, mi Capitan.*"

Castillo returned the salute and the soldier exited. "The men are ready, Sam. We better hurry."

"Give me a minute to say goodbye, will you?"

Castillo smiled and offered an exaggerated bow, then said quietly, "Of course...it might be best if *señor* Jim stayed in town for a few days. No, Sam? We'll start boarding the boats."

Castillo give Jim a friendly salute and left.

Sam and Jim stood quietly, watching the police officer disappear through the swinging doors.

"What the hell's going on?" Jim asked in a rushed whisper.

Sam turned to Carmen, the local tart with whom he stood. "Hey, toots," he said with a smile, "time to hit the road."

"You don't tell me to leave so quick last night," she pursed her lips and looked at him side-ways.

"There'll be other nights, darlin'. Right now, I gotta' talk to Jim...alone."

The men waited as she drifted down the bar to find a new patron. "It's Snake Ghost," Sam said quietly, "the army thinks he's prowling the mountain country."

The news made Jim instantly concerned. He knew who Snake Ghost was. Everyone did. A legendary figure. A marauder who led a gang of merciless head-hunters. He worked for the slavers who supplied the rubber plantations with labor. Seldom seen, Snake Ghost had developed a reputation for stealth and cruelty, and to have him reported in the area around Jim's home was seriously dangerous.

Jim shook his head, "What would he be doing up there?" he wondered aloud. "That's the thickest part of the jungle. Almost no one lives up that way—it's no good for slaving."

Sam spoke while filling his hip flask from the bottle at the bar. "Beats me, but the army wants to catch him or kill him... either way, it'll be bloody. Maybe you *should* stay in town for a few days; you can use my room upstairs."

Jim looked worried. "Sammy, lad, be careful. You know what the natives say about the highlands?"

Sam smiled, "You mean curi-puri, the haunted jungle." He threw down another drink, then tapped Jim on the stomach. "Come on, don't tell me an old altar boy like you is scared of some old native superstition."

"It's no joke, boyo—I've felt it meself and so have you. You're just too brave or dumb to admit it...anyway, up there it's stronger, and you know it."

"Jimmy, if I can see it, I can kill it...and if I can't see it...then it doesn't bother me. I gotta go pal, be careful." Sam pulled a keyring from his pocket and handed it to Jim.

Jim affectionately pushed the key away, "If I'm to die, I'll do it in me own bed. May the road be good to you, Sam."

Jim watched Sam swagger out of the bar, and feeling a sudden chill, shook his head and crossed himself. Curi-puri was one of those things that nobody could describe, but everybody agreed was real—some kind of force that ran thick through the jungle. A primal awareness behind an unseen hand that touched events. However you felt about it, it was something you didn't want to fool with.

Chapter 3

The big black limo navigated traffic through the brick canyons of downtown New York, where dreary hordes of people wandered, zombie-like, through gloomy banks of exhaust fog.

Tom and Linda sat in the back, snug and warm against the plush gray mole-skin upholstery. She spoke excitedly, and he was looking at her more than listening as she explained her reasoning.

"So, in really thinking about it, it became very simple. You see, Truman has to be either alive or dead... if he's alive, then they can't cut me off, and if he's dead, then I should share in the estate per his will. Either way, they'll have to pay me something." Her right fist pounded into her left palm, as she nodded to herself and rolled her head and faced Tom.

He noted everything, how her face was beautifully framed between the fox fur stole above her black wool coat and the dark rounded shape of the small black cloche hat that almost covered her hair, leaving only a tiny curl to spill across her forehead. How her large eyes, outlined with dark mascara, contrasted with her full, luscious lips, a moist tomato red—both augmenting her smooth pale, rice-powered skin.

My God. She's amazing, Tom thought to himself, as her fragrance surrounded him. *She smells like geraniums and baby-powder.*

"Well?"

Tom saw her waiting for an answer of some kind.

"What do you think?" Her brows arched, and Tom wished he had followed her childish ramblings more closely.

He smiled, unable to think of a satisfactory answer.

Linda turned away, crushed back in her seat, and looked out her window. "You weren't listening," she said in a small, disappointed voice.

Tom felt rescued when the limo pulled to the curb in front of a large office building.

Tom and Linda looked from the car window to see the polished brass plaque that read, "World Rubber Company".

· · · ● · ● · · ·

"Don't worry," said Tom, as he opened the door, stepping to the curb, and extending his hand to help her from the limousine. "I'll handle everything. You just sit there and look beautiful—although a few tears might help," he suggested.

Linda stepped to the sidewalk, pulling her coat closer against the windy chill of the street.

Suddenly, her attention was caught by the ragged figure of an approaching street girl selling apples. Linda felt a pang of recognition in the girl's sad eyes, making her suddenly uncomfortable. She recognized despair and hopelessness; happiness crushed out of the youthful face by poverty. Linda suddenly experienced a clutch of cold fear for herself and her own future.

Will I be destitute too? she wondered.

Quickly, she stopped and searched her purse. Retrieving some change, she handed the girl a quarter, enough for five apples, and left before receiving them.

They crossed the sidewalk to the polished brass and thick glass front doors.

"That's great," smiled Tom, as a doorman allowed them entry.

She had a moment's pause, trying to understand Tom's comment.

"The tears," he smiled into her luminous eyes, "that's great, really great. How do you do that? Oh, I suppose it's a stage thing."

They crossed the large marble lobby, ornately decorated with gold framed mosaics, and entered the elevator while the uniformed elevator operator held the art déco grillwork door open for them.

She quickly felt powerless. Her jaw flexed with a kind of nervous twitch and fought not to bite her thumb. *Well, I'm here now, and I have to go through with it*, she thought, even as a knot tightened in her stomach.

She felt a weightless bounce as the floor stopped under her feet.

The elevator boy opened the grate, smiled, and bowed and said, "Top floor, chairman's office."

Tom led her down the carpeted hall, past large portraits of dour looking men, toward a pair of impressively decorated doors guarded by a well-dressed woman who sat, mannequin still, behind an enormous hand-carved desk.

Tom spoke in a soft, almost reverential tone, "Tom Jackman and Linda Dawson for the Chairman."

Linda watched as the woman gave her an appraising but suitably disinterested look, then smiled at Tom, nodded, and said, "Go right in, Mister Jackman. He's expecting you."

Tom held the door for Linda, and she entered first into a large, paneled conference room, a room that was bigger than the farmhouse she had grown up in. She crossed the plush carpet between the potted palms in tall Chinese vases to find herself a chair at a table long enough to seat fifty. A white-jacketed attendant pulled the chair for her as the chairman and his lawyers stood, smiled vacantly, and extended hands to Tom, who shook politely before sitting. Tom, Linda, and the chairman, flanked by two company lawyers, sat across the table from one another in a room quietly charged with electricity.

"You don't mind if I smoke," said the chairman, more a statement than a question.

"No, of course not," Tom smiled as the chairman's cigar was lit by another white jacketed attendant.

"It's a *Grande Numero Uno*, Cuban. Want a drink?" the chairman waved with a rolling hand motion.

"No, thank you, perhaps after we conclude," Tom issued in a velvet voice.

"How about the little lady?" said the Chairman, taking a few shallow puffs, his narrow eyes riveted on Linda, boring into her, "Mrs. Dawson I mean."

Tom was impressed. He could see that the chairman was setting the stage for a tough negotiation-good, that meant that they were concerned.

"Tom says that you have something to say to us, that right?"

Linda nodded, a little too weakly, "Yes, yes, I do."

"Well? Go ahead."

Linda gulped down her intimidation; then, under the stony gaze of the powerful men surrounding her, she advanced her argument point by point, careful not to leave anything out. In the end she sat back, trying to hide her nervousness, afraid they would see the slight trembling she could feel, the cigar smoke adding to her discomfort.

The company men conferred. They turned to each other and spoke quietly, finally nodding back and forth in agreement. The chairman then leaned back in his chair to the sound of squeaking leather as the three stony figures scowled from across the table.

The chairman's eyes were small, dark, and cold. He took a long pull from his cigar and blew a tall stream of bluish smoke skyward as he said softly, "Nope. Nothing."

Linda blanched in disbelief, jolted upright, repeating, "Nothing? What do you mean, nothing?!" Her wide eyes searching from one impassive face to the next.

The chairman shook his thumb at the first lawyer, who turned a pencil in his hands end over end, never quite facing her as he answered, "You see, Truman, your husband, is ahh, missing. Neither dead nor alive. Ahh, legally speaking, we have no authorization to support his estranged wife," he waved the pencil in little circles, "nor can we ahh, administer his will without proof of his demise.... We can only run the business." He shrugged helplessly, looked away, and tossed the pencil into the silence that followed.

Linda's mind raced. "What kind of proof do you need?" A slight hopefulness clinging to her words.

The lawyers conferred again, whispering and nodding, shielding their mouths as they spoke, then satisfied in their agreement, they sat back and turned to face her.

The second lawyer cleared his throat for attention, adjusted his glasses to look down his nose, then uttered through his pinched lips, "His remains preferably."

They nodded in unison.

Linda took a breath as she looked from one impassive expression to another. They reminded her of the little Chinese carving of three monkeys that Truman had: Deaf, Dumb, and Blind.

"Great," she asked sarcastically, sitting back and folding her arms. "Anything else?"

Tom entered the conversation tentatively. "A notarized certificate of death, perhaps?" Some musing followed, then, "Properly documented by local authority, of course."

The chairman chimed in, "We'd require a verifiable attachment from a coroner, including an autopsy report certifying cause of death for insurance purposes."

Lawyer number one added his opinion, "It will all go to court, anyway." He tossed his pencil on the desk again.

"Any statutes of limitations?" queried Tom.

"About seven years I would guess," opined lawyer number two, nodding his thin head.

Linda jumped from her seat, her intimidation now swept away on a tide of anger. She held the marble edge of the table with both of her gloved hands. "Seven years!" She looked at the men's icy stares. "You crooks!" she said through clenched teeth.

The chairman, unmoved, shrugged. "Sue us," he said, tapping dead ash from his cigar into a silver tray.

Stifling a sob, Linda turned and rushed for the door, stopping long enough to turn back and say, "Your cigar smells like crap."

They watched her leave.

The doors closed behind her. Tom stood. "Excuse me, gentlemen, I'll be right back." He exchanged professional smiles and handshakes with the others.

Outside, Tom caught Linda in the hall by the elevators—found her crying, dabbing at her eyes with a handkerchief. "You mustn't get emotional...it's only business, nothing personal."

Linda turned on Tom, mascara tear tracks on her cheeks. "Nothing personal? Only business? You know I don't have a lot of money saved, Tom. I'll be starving soon. That's pretty personal!"

Tom held her gloved hands gently. He looked into her eyes with professional sincerity, "It'll never get that bad. Take the car. Go home. Wait. I'll come over later, we'll have dinner... talk...we'll figure something out. I'll never let you starve." He smiled, handsome and perfect in his dark morning clothes and silk foulard.

She managed a weak smile. "I have to do something, Tom. I'm running out of hope."

He tried to give her a consoling hug. She pushed away.

Tom watched her get into the elevator, then headed back to the board room, retaking his seat with a faint smile, knowing that things could now get serious with her gone as an audience.

The chairman spoke first, "Well?"

"She's determined...entitled even...she could have a pretty good case."

"What do you suggest?" asked the chairman, his pinched expression showing concern as he looked down and drew money signs on the legal pad in front of him.

"I suggest you pay her something."

"I disagree, it'll set a bad precedent," opined lawyer number two, suddenly roused.

"Hmmm," mused the chairman. "Get her off our back, huh? Not a bad idea. Why not come to dinner tonight and discuss it...there might be a bright future here for all of us..."

The chairman reached across the table and patted Tom's hand. Tom beamed. The two house-lawyers were stony faced.

"Glad to. After all, Truman and the company is our mutual primary interest...incidentally, any news from the Iquitos office on him?"

"Not so far. Seems Truman really just disappeared. The only reports are confusing. They say he was doing something that he was very secretive about and...just walked away from everything. What's worse, it seems he started freeing the plantation slaves and now the whole country's in an uproar, even the police—"

"I thought the police stayed out of company business," interrupted Tom, afraid of the effects that bad publicity might have on the company's stock value in his portfolio.

"As long as we keep things peaceful...anyway, we have men out looking for him right now."

"Plantation guards?"

"Er...no, not exactly—more of a...private force."

The three company men conferred with their eyes.

Tom saw through the veneer and decided not to know too much, adding, "If there's a chance of anything going wrong...we have to preserve a discrete distance, you know, plausible deniability."

"Oh, I wouldn't worry too much about that. These fellows aren't the kind to leave much of a paper trail."

Smiles were exchanged all around the table.

"Brandy?" asked the chairman as he rose and snuffed his cigar, "She's right, these things do smell like crap."

Everyone laughed.

Chapter 4

A small jungle village nestled in a clearing surrounded by thick greenery and tall mountains. All was quiet except for the sound of a close waterfall. An Indian brave lazed in a hammock fletching an arrow.

Suddenly, a camp bird gave a startled cry. The brave looked up and was blown from his hammock by a shotgun blast.

The village was thrown into a panic as shots and arrows were fired from the close brush. Strangely painted savages shouted war cries and rushed from cover to attack. Indians grappled in brutal hand to hand combat...but the village was no match for the raiders.

The shooting died down as the last of the villagers were killed or captured.

Armed men stepped into the clearing, including Snake Ghost, medicine man/war chief, blood-thirsty savage, covered with red and black painted designs, shrunken heads hanging from his trophy belt. The leader, Carascas, mid-forties, heavy-

set, and cruel eyed, wore the dirty threadbare remains of a tropical suit and the haunted expression of a hunted animal. Soto,
big, greasy—with a glint of perversity behind his red-rimmed
eyes. And Juanito, Soto's younger brother, who moved with
a kind of jumpy nervousness that marked him as a cowardly
scavenger.

The war party began to butcher the fallen villagers amid the
cries of the survivors. Juanito looked away. "We shouldn't bother with this."

"Why not?" shrugged Carascas, "The men have to eat. Besides, we have time."

"We should stay on his trail." Juanito rejoined, nodding to the
surrounding mountains and the wet green jungle that faded up
into grey mist.

"He's right, *hermanito*. There's no rush. That gringo is dead
meat by now," said Soto.

"What's he doing up here, anyway?" questioned Juanito.

"*Esta loco*," came Soto's answer.

"No. He's not crazy. They wouldn't pay us to find a crazy
man. He's alone...he don't got nothing...so he must know
something, something worth a lot of money, I think—"

A woman screamed. Soto lit up with a ghoulish grin and led
Juanito and Snake Ghost away.

Carascas stood alone, thinking. He rubbed the stubble on his
chin as he gazed into the thick greenery and across the distant
grey mountains shrouded mysteriously in dark low-hanging
clouds.

"What is it, *gringo*? What do you know? What are you after?" he asked himself, wondering what all this trouble would really be worth in the end.

• • • ●• ●• • •

Night surrounded the Truman mansion. Inside, Linda, beautiful in a silver Harlow gown, descended the grand staircase and was greeted by the smiling face of Williams, the family's old retainer. In all the years of service to Truman, the last two years with Linda as "mistress" had been the best. Her kindness and humor had won the respect of everyone who worked at The Gardens.

"Man, oh man...you look like an angel coming down from heaven," he said, meaning it.

"Thanks, Williams. I know you're lying, but I can use it...has Mister Jackman called?"

"Yes ma'am, 'bout an hour ago. He said not to disturb you. Said he'd be busy tonight but would be by tomorrow."

"Oh..."

"But that pot roast is looking good for two or for one...can I serve you some dinner? You look a little peek-id."

"No thanks. I'm not very hungry. Why don't you and Sarah take the night off—and take that pot roast with you."

"You sure?"

"I'm sure. I'm tired. I think I'll go to bed early, thanks."

"Thank you, Miss Linda. Say..."

"Yes?"

"Well, me and Sarah, that is, well, we just want you to know that we'll be praying that the good Lord will see you through all this trouble."

"Thank you, Williams," she said, genuinely touched. "I think I'm going to need all the help I can get."

"Well, you gonna get all the help you need, and you can stand on that. I know because God gave you the shiniest smile I ever saw, so it just stands to reason that He don't want to see it buried under a lot of misery…"

She gave Williams a hug. "He'll have to send me a big, tough angel…"

"And a handsome one, too, if you ask nice…" a warm smile spread across his face.

She couldn't help but laugh. "Maybe I'll do that. Goodnig ht…"

"Goodnight…"

Williams crossed to the kitchen, his footsteps fading on the marble tile, leaving Linda alone.

She felt the quiet. The house was grand. Everywhere she looked was marble, gold, Turkish carpets, Impressionist paintings, Japanese vases full of fresh-cut flowers, Louis XV, or Chinese Chippendale furniture. Everything was beautiful, but the hollow echo of Williams's footfall betrayed the home's true nature. It was dead. For all its beauty and expensive ornamentation, it was a mausoleum, a loveless homage to wealth.

She had tried to make it a home, to make it more comfortable by suggesting warmer colors to replace the business-like lead greys that Truman preferred. He had resisted all her attempts, save a few vases filled with flowers from their garden. So, she had thrown herself into gardening, working outside with the groundskeeper she planted, and potted, and pruned, and raised beds of lively color to give the house a friendly floral ambiance year-round.

She had tried in other ways as well. She delighted in preparing meals, working in the kitchen with Sarah. Delighted in small-talk and trading recipes. Just as she worked with Williams in preparing the lavish dinners for friends of Truman.

But all these activities, born of good intentions and hard work, never bore the fruit of happiness. They seemed instead to become contentious, to anger Truman. He had told her he didn't want to marry a domestic servant, and that just keeping herself attractive was enough. That's when she realized he didn't want a wife, not really. He wanted a living jewel for his crown of wealth. A showpiece, a prop. She was a living piece of furniture to decorate the opulent trophy-room that was his life.

Linda ambled down the hall and opened the doors of Truman's expansive den. Inside, it was all cherry wood, leather, and marble, lit by a crackling fire and not much else. It was crowded with books, trophies, and artifacts that bespoke of a life of adventure and travel. The room was dominated by a large oil painting of a younger but resolute Truman Dawson, scowling down from above the mantle, hanging in a platinum frame.

She regarded the portrait as she scooped up a bottle of brandy from a silver butler's tray. Standing before the fire, she held the bottle up in a mock toast.

"Here's to you, Truman. You jerk!" She took a deep swig.

Then, expelling a hot sigh, she turned to the pool table, where she put the bottle down and picked up a pool cue. Stalking the table, she began shooting a half-hearted game of pool while pulling at the brandy and carrying on an angry one-way conversation with Truman's impassive portrait.

"Oh Truman, you jerk. Why are you doing this to me? I did everything I could to make it work. You never wanted a wife," she slammed a ball across the table, "you just wanted a trophy for your bedroom. God, men...if a girl marries rich, she's a gold digger—if she marries poor, she's stupid—if she has sex for money, she's a whore—if she does it for free, she's a slut."

She shot hard again, heard the smack of the balls, and saw the eight ball bounce off the table. She followed it across the Turkish carpet.

"If she likes it, she's a nympho; if she doesn't, she's frigid."

Linda stopped at the desk, bent down for the ball, and came face to face with a small gold statue on the corner of the desk. The idol seemed to mock her with upraised hands and a wide smile.

"What ever happened to love? That's all I ever wanted." She picked up the statue, looked at it...spoke to it. "Men don't want love, they want stuff. Well, I don't want love anymore either. I want stuff too, green stuff, and lots of it!"

She turned angrily and hurled the statue at Truman's portrait. The painting ripped and jumped as the statue hit Truman's face and shattered on the wall behind. Linda covered her eyes reflexively as something flew off the mantle and landed at her feet—she looked—it was an old book—gleaming in the firelight, small, dark and dog-eared from years of handling. The title was in gold embossed letters, now faint but readable, TEARS

OF THE SUN, EL DORADO AND OTHER LOST INCA TREASURES.

Linda stooped and slowly picked it up, eyeing it tentatively as she stood. The fire cracked and popped, and the shadows danced around her as she stared at the cover—her finger tracing the title as she whispered to herself softly, "Is that it Truman? Is that where you've gone? After treasure?"

Her eyes narrowed with suspicion, as a faint smile played on her lips. She took a comfortable seat behind Truman's large desk, and turned on the reading lamp.

Chapter 5

Late the next afternoon, Williams answered a knock at the front door with his usual smile. "Morning, Mister Tom."

"Morning, Williams," Tom said, handing over a large bouquet of flowers, "tell Mrs. Dawson I'm here, will you?"

"She's gone out, Mister Tom. Left early this morning. Said she was going to the movies, then had some shopping to do. Said you should wait. Have a drink if you want to."

Williams led Tom into the den, where Tom saw the destroyed portrait. "Good heavens, what happened?"

"I asked her if she was shooting up the place last night, but she said that her and Mister Truman was just having an argument …"

"An argument?"

"Yes, sir. Sure looks like he lost too…first time I seen her smile in days. 'Scuse me while I get some water," he said with a slight bow, as he turned and headed for the kitchen, leaving Tom free to exercise his curiosity and inspect the damage.

It wasn't long before Tom reacted to the sound of a car horn. Out the window he could see a taxi, and Linda, the driver, and Williams, all struggling with store wrapped boxes.

Tom scanned the room, leaving nothing unnoticed. He fingered the near empty brandy bottle, then stopped at a mirror to adjust his tie, and slick back his hair, as an excited Linda entered with Williams, both loaded with store bags and packages.

"Ah, Linda…" He said cheerfully.

"Hi, Tom," she answered flatly.

Tom, wearing a Cheshire cat smile, reached for his inside coat pocket, clearing his throat for effect, but Linda was too busy unpacking to notice. She started holding up new clothes, skirts, shirts, breeches, all in olive, and khaki.

"Hey, stop that for a minute and listen," he said as he slid a folded paper from his coat and held it up. "The company wants you to sign this," he pronounced, smiling with smug anticipation.

"What is it?" she asked unconcerned, clothes and wrapping paper still flying.

Tom, the air let out of his announcement, couldn't suppress his frustration. "Well, they agreed with me…it took some real negotiating, I can tell you, but in the end, they're ready to settle. Isn't that great?" he said, curiosity rising, realizing he only had half her attention, if that.

"Maybe. What's their offer?" asked Linda, extricating a bush jacket from package wrappings.

"A hundred and fifty dollars a week until your death or the company changes hands—" Tom said triumphantly.

"What do you think?" she said, holding up the khaki jacket.

"Quite generous under the circumstances."

"I mean the jacket, you lunk."

"Fine, I guess. Say, what is all this?" He let the paper fall to his side.

"What if I told you that I know where Truman is?" She gushed excitedly.

"You do?"

"Maybe," she said coyly, continuing to unpack.

"I don't think you should waste any time. They might change their minds," he said, sounding the faintest bit desperate.

"Well, maybe I've changed my mind!" She spoke with defiance as she threw the jacket down, then searched for another piece of clothing.

"Hey, what's gotten into you?" Tom asked, stepping forward, his curiosity piqued.

"It's a secret. I'll tell you when I get back," Linda said, still unwrapping packages.

"From more shopping?"

"From South America." She waved away the question.

"What?" Tom felt caught off-guard. This had nothing to do with the plans he was carefully orchestrating with the company.

"I'm finishing up the details right now."

Tom looked at the safari clothes with a new understanding. She was acting impulsively again. Getting ready to do something without his consultation and outside his control.

"Oh, no..." he said, in a paternal tone, "I'm not letting you traipse off on some wild goose chase through that god-forsaken country. Why, you could get yourself killed."

She turned on him, jaw flexing. "Really? Just how do you plan to stop me? Look, I'm using the last of my money, I'm doing my research, and planning for everything. Besides, if Truman likes it down there, how dangerous can it be?"

· · · ● · ● · ● · · ·

Carascas, Soto, Juanito and their men gained the top of a thickly forested rise. Below them stretched a long narrow valley that snaked away to be lost in the blur of distant mountains.

They had stopped here because of the Indian sign. Above them stood a line of human skulls hoisted on long bamboo poles. Even Snake Ghost looked apprehensive, as did his silent gang of green and black painted head-hunters.

"This is no good, *hermano*," said Juanito, already recoiling at the dank air, his hands nervously wringing his rifle stock.

"We got to," said Carascas gruffly. "The trackers said the gringo went down there." He pointed, indicating the faint trail that led into the valley below. "So, we got to go down there after him." He fingered his pistol. "And I don't want no arguments."

After some hesitation, they slithered down the steep muddy track, and into the swampy mulch that was the valley floor. They stopped at dusk to make camp.

The up-land vegetation had changed with the altitude, more brush and tall canopied trees and fewer broad-leafed plants and palms. The weather also was different, less humidity and more cooling breezes from the surrounding snowcapped mountains.

'They built a fire as night closed in on them, shuddering at the unexpected drop in temperature. Snake Ghost and his men were particularly edgy and uncomfortable, being more accustomed to the riverine flatlands they called home.

The night was spent uneasily as new animal sounds assaulted them. Heavy grunting and deep growling seemed to surround them. Things they had never heard before in the low-lands, dangerous sounding unknown things that unnerved even the head-hunters. And, there were the bones. Rib bones, leg bones, crushed pelvises—a perfusion of naked bone fragments poked up, here and there, from the dark, wet earth.

• • • ● •● •● • •• ••

The next morning, they gathered around the smoldering remains of their campfire. The men were still uneasy in the mist-bound stillness. The silence was broken only by the familiar echoes of screeching monkeys and early bird calls.

"We've lost him. Let's turn back." Juanito said plaintively, "This place is cursed. Everyone feels it."

Carascas glanced around at the head-hunters. They were huddled together in a group for warmth, shivering and talking among themselves. They had been nervous since passing the skull signs the day before. Now they looked ready to desert.

"Shut up," he said finally.

"Well, I'm going back." Juanito threw a stick into the fire as he stood.

"You're going nowhere. Not 'til we find him." Carascas said as he reached for the pistol in his waistband.

Juanito looked around, his face wearing a panicked expression. "You stay if you want," he said. "I'm not going to die in this god-forsaken place for some crazy gringo."

"BLAM!" A gunshot exploded from the bush and Juanito's body was thrown through the damp smoke and into the hot coals.

The camp erupted into confused action as Carascas and his men began trading shots with Sam and the soldiers who continued shooting from ambush.

The soldier next to Sam was hit. Sam rushed to scoop up the wounded man's Lewis gun, then stood and shouted, "Come on, men, you want to live forever?" while he charged the bandits, dashing across broken ground, firing a chattering volley from the hip.

A shout went up from the soldiers and they followed him in a mad attack. Snake Ghost and the headhunters not killed in the first volley ducked away quickly, vanishing into the shadows, leaving Carascas and his few men to fight alone—but the force of the charge scattered the bandits.

Carascas turned, blood running from a facial wound, and fired at Sam, the bullet chipping bark close to his head, then he turned and ducked into the jungle and disappeared.

The last few shots fired, the soldiers regrouped in the clearing filled with dead bodies and the gun-smoke that still hung in the air.

Sam handed the Lewis gun to a grinning soldier as he pulled his hip flask and took a drink. The men laughed and cheered, taking turns slapping each other on the back. Sam walked to where Castillo knelt, checking Juanito's smoldering body.

There was a heavy growl, quiet but close. Sam's ears perked up. "You hear that?" he said.

"What?"

"Something's out there," Sam breathed, his eyes scanning the dense undergrowth.

Castillo listened a moment, "Maybe wild pigs. They get very large up here..." Then turning back to the body, "This is Juanito, Soto's little brother. He'll be very mad at you."

"He can stand in line."

A soldier ran up, out of breath and nervous. "*Mi Capitan. Ya esta ruenas, muy cerca.*"

"*Seguro?*" said Castillo.

"*Si, de mucho antigueos.*"

"He said there are some old ruins..."

"Yeah, I heard," said Sam.

Castillo stood, brushing off his knees, "Come on, let's have a look."

There was another growl.

"Damn, did you hear that?" asked Sam, unheard by the others as they drifted away, overcome with curiosity in their new discovery.

Sam could not shake his uneasiness at the dangerous animal sound he had never heard before, but he followed the men as they moved up the jungle trail into the ground-fog and cool early morning shadows.

Ahead, the soldiers had stopped. They had collected, and stood in a group, staring. There, before them, stood a large carved stone gate, vine covered, obscured, but recognizable.

Castillo drew a machete and cleared the tendril vines.

Sam continued to look around, searching for whatever might be the source of the sound that was still making him nervous.

As the sun rose, dispelling the grey gloom, new shafts of warm light spread under the canopy, revealing more ruins, the remains of an ancient fallen city.

"What the hell is this place?" asked Sam.

"I've never seen anything like it," came Castillo's reply.

The soldiers murmured among themselves. Sam took another drink. "What's wrong with them?" he asked Castillo, jerking a thumb towards the soldiers.

"They want to go back. They think this place is full of evil spirits, ghosts, haunted."

"More of that curi-puri stuff, huh?"

"Not too loud, Sam. They believe in it."

"Well, it's time they stopped!"

Sam looked around. A few feet away, half buried in the foliage, lay a large, overturned statue of a grinning god. Sam pulled another drink and hopped up on the reclining statue. The soldiers shrank back in superstitious fear as Sam flashed a wrinkled grin and pushed his battered campaign hat back on his head, "Now, look here, men" he said, putting his hands on his hips, "You can't let this kind of stuff scare you." He stamped his foot on the face of the fallen idol.

The soldiers gasped and took another step back.

Castillo became nervous. "Sam?"

But Sam was enjoying himself. "Gods and ghosts are for other people, not us." He jerked his thumb at himself. "We're soldiers," he thumped his chest, "and a soldier can only believe in two things, his rifle and himself. Why, any man who can't believe in himself is a coward and not fit for human company."

He scanned the Indian faces of the soldiers and realized that his appeal was making no inroads into their fears or antiquated superstitions.

"Here, I'll show you," he said, still grinning, and tipped his flask again as the soldiers nervously retreated a few more steps.

Castillo waved his hand for Sam to stop, "Sam, come down from there. The men are afraid."

"Jeez, that's what I'm talking about...look, I'll show you." He grinned as he reached down and unbuttoned his fly, terrifying the soldiers even more.

"SAM!" shouted Castillo.

But Sam was grinning like a schoolboy as he urinated on the idol—laughing as a trickle of water ran down the stone face.

Shouting in panic, the soldiers broke and ran...threw down their rifles and sprinted into the surrounding dark bush.

"Sam! Stop!" Castillo yelled as he turned and ran into the undergrowth after the fleeing soldiers.

Sam, laughing, took another drink as he hopped down off the statue. He could hear soldiers yelling and splashing through the water. Still grinning, he followed them into the thick undergrowth, shaking his head at their cowardice.

"Hey guys, come on back...there's nothing—"

Suddenly, the jungle exploded with cries and yells, growls, roars, and terrifying shrieks.

Sam blanched. He stared into the trembling jungle, unable to move.

Something heavy hit him in the chest, knocking him down ...he looked...Castillo's bloody head sat in his lap, grimacing a dead grin, sightless eyes staring up in silent rebuke.

Sam's face froze in a mask of horror. Instantly flooded with panic, he shouted breathlessly and scrambled away from the lifeless head and the sounds of carnage, from the terrified cries, the trembling jungle and the roaring growls that were now all around him, reverberating through his body and robbing his mind of sanity.

He ran heedlessly, unable to stop, crashing and stumbling, propelled by the fear that had consumed him.

He finally collapsed, exhausted, at the top of the ridge, under the cluster of skulls that still swayed on bamboo poles, empty eye sockets staring at him, jaws hanging open in contemptuous silent laughter.

Muddy and soiled, his hands clutched at the wet earth, he trembled and sobbed drunkenly. He had been arrogant, and the jungle had taught him the truth. The truth was that he was a coward, and now the jungle had spit him out.

Chapter 6

Tom was surprised by the call from the chairman's office. He was wanted for a meeting without Linda.

He wondered the reason as he sat across from the same three lawyers who had met with him before.

The chairman tossed a dirty envelope addressed to Tom Jackman across the table. "Well, go on, open it."

Tom picked up the soiled envelope, turned it in his hands. "Where did it come from?"

"Our Iquitos office. Now open it."

Tom opened the envelope, unfolded the letter with the slow teasing grace of a fan-dancer. "Hmm." He mused, smiling.

"What the hell is that supposed to mean? What does it say?" demanded the chairman.

"Not returning. Leave everything to wife Linda... signed Truman—"

"Here, let me see that."

Tom handed the letter across the table. The company men huddled over it, read it, exchanged dour looks, then fell into a worried silence.

"Well, what do you make of it?"

"It appears to mean that my employer, our employer, is instructing me to transfer the ownership of all his worldly possessions and estates, including this company, to his wife," said Tom.

"Why, you can't do that!" the chairman croaked, sitting forward, and banging a fist on the table.

Tom thrilled. "That's incorrect. I can do that. The more tantalizing question is, will I?" Tom sat back, templed his hands, allowed a slight upturn of his lips, something just short of a smile.

The table fell quiet. Tom regarded the moment as a high-stakes poker game. This letter had dealt him a flush, and he sat across from three-of-a-kind. The question now was how to bet.

The chairman tossed the letter back, feigning unconcern. "Why, look at this thing. It could have been written by anybody," waving his hand over it, as if to make it disappear.

"May be a forgery," exclaimed lawyer number one.

"May have been written under duress, or, or, he might not have been in charge of his mental faculties," nodded lawyer number two.

"Yes, yes, and it may be a deathbed request and constitute a legal will change, or he might still be alive and mean it. The point is, we don't know." Tom sat back, sensing they were about to fold. The first thing to do was to stall a little, seek out any other information. "Any new news on Truman?" he asked, trying to hold back his growing excitement.

"Our men lost him in the jungle," said the dispirited chairman, with a telltale drop of the eyes.

Tom let the silence hang for a while. Then, "Linda wants to go to the Amazon," he tapped the envelope on the table for emphasis.

"What?" The chairman's eyes came up alertly, "Do you think she knows something?"

"I'm not sure, but she thinks she does. In any event, it's clear she needs some, ahh, full-time legal guidance...a sympathetic confidant, so to speak."

"So, you aren't going to tell her about the letter? You're going along to help console the poor woman? Anything about the ethics of that bother you?"

Tom shrugged, "Why should it, after all, it's the least I can do...she may well be the most eligible bachelorette in America. I wouldn't want to see her...assets...fall into the wrong hands." He looked at his beautifully manicured nails.

"Yes, we've all noticed her beautiful...assets. It seems to me, Tom," said the chairman, leaning forward, a smile of conspiracy illuminating his eyes, "that beneath that suave exterior of yours, there crouches an ambitious and dangerous animal that's prepared to overcome any obstacle in a ruthless pursuit of its own self-interest." The chairman leaned back, "Frankly, I like that about you.... Now, let's get real." His eyes narrowed and his tone dropped as he crouched forward. "You go with her and watch what happens; and when the time comes, make whatever appropriate decision is necessary to benefit our mutual interests. Agreed?"

Tom silently watched his opportunities carousel for a moment: everyone, Linda, the company management, were bobbing around on a sea of uncertainty. Only he was on the firm footing of solid information, he knew his interests and possessed Truman's letter for leverage. "In other words, you want me to, ah, represent her interests with a determined lack of vigor," his mouth smiled, his eyes didn't.

The chairman leaned back, comfortable for the first time in the meeting, "That's indelicately blunt, but not without a certain degree of insightfulness."

"Your interests are plain enough to see, but what exactly might my interests be?" queried Tom.

"You seem like the kind of team player we might need around here. How about a vice president's chair? Name your own salary. Stock options, corner suite, maybe even a shot at political office. Ever seen the governor's mansion?"

"And if any of this becomes...problematic...for Linda?" Tom let the question hang in the stillness. Lawyers one and two swiveled their heads around as if they hadn't heard anything.

"We'll leave it to you, Tom, to, ahh...plumb the depths of her conundrum."

· · · ● · ● · · ·

Tom considered his course of action carefully as he was driven to Truman's estate and to a confrontation with Linda. His objectives were tempered by complicating circumstances. If he revealed Truman's letter too soon, the game would be over, and he would find himself at cross-purposes in what was sure to be a lengthy lawsuit. If his concealment of the letter was discovered, he could say that he withheld the information awaiting more substantial conformation, not wanting to inflate Linda's hopes prematurely.

The thing now was to stall her a little, gain more information, enough to suggest a sound plan for dealing with eventualities and, most importantly, stay in control of the situation.

He found Linda in the study, standing over two packed suitcases.

"Linda, I've been thinking..." he started.

"Don't bother, I've carefully planned everything to the last detail and made all the arrangements. I'm taking a steamer to Lima, then an airplane to...to where I'm going."

"Where's that?"

"Never mind, I'm keeping my cat in the bag until I find Truman. Sorry, Tom, but that goes for you too."

"Hmmm," Tom mumbled, pursing his lips.

He leaned back, watching her, thinking fast. He saw it was too late to dissuade her, and although he disliked making quick decisions, much less impulsive ones—only fools did that, and he wasn't a fool—it seemed immediate action was required, and there seemed to be only one solution to maintain control and stay in a superior position. "Alright then, I'll go with you," he announced.

"No, Tom—"

"Yes, Linda. You don't know what kind of dangers you'll face, regardless of your planning, and if you do need help, you won't be able to count on anyone. No Linda, I'm not taking 'no' for an answer. Now then, when do we leave?"

· · · **·** · **·** · · ·

The sun had already dropped below the line of western mountains known as the Cordilleras, but another hour of fading blue light remained.

Jim's hut still rested quietly along the green tributary, with two canoes tied to the landing.

Sam and Jim sat at a small table, a bottle between them. Both men were silent. Jim was uncomfortable. Sam looked pale and washed out, even in the warm amber oil lamp light.

"Well, whatever happened, laddie, it wasn't your fault. You can't take it so hard," said Jim, trying to console his friend.

"No, it's over for me, Jim. Don't you understand? The jungle's through with me."

"Aww, we all lose it sometimes, boyo...." Jim's stomach turned uneasily. Sam had always been a pillar of strength and courage. To see him like this, dispirited and fearful, was worse than seeing him dead.

"Not like this," Sam went on, "I broke and ran like a scared rabbit." He banged his fist on the table, then rubbed the shivers from his arms at the memory. "I lost my nerve. Without nerve, a man's no good in this country. I gotta get out."

Sam threw down a drink. His haunted stare made Jim look away.

"Where will ye go, laddie, and how? Bush rats like us ain't got much money."

"I've saved a little. I'll canoe to the mission, then to the plantation at Las Crusas. Try to catch a ride back to Peru or Venezuela with J.J.'s plane—if he doesn't show, I'll walk out."

"That's over three hundred tough miles away," Jim said as he leaned back, thinking of the dangerous, almost impossible journey Sam was describing for his trip. "Why not wait for the mail boat? What if the headhunters start to rampage? You'll be surrounded by danger and alone."

Jim stopped. He could read the defeat in Sam's posture. He went on, pleading his concern, "Why can't you just stay here with me till you feel better, or wait in Iquitos?"

It took a moment for Sam's head to come up. "Nah, I don't have the heart for it anymore. There's nothing for me here. Hell, there's nothing for me anywhere. I just want to get going."

Sam looked up and Jim saw his hollow, sunken eyes, and swallowed.

Chapter 7

A tramp steamer plowed the calm Caribbean under a beautiful star-filled sky. Dance music from the ship's Victrola filled the evening air, along with the sound of a girl's laughter.

The few passengers and ship officers dined together. There was the charming, elegant feeling of tuxedos, evening gowns and dress whites mixed with silver service, polished mahogany, and oil lamp light.

Tom spoke to the officer next to him, while Linda sat in a world of her own. All eyes were on the young honeymoon couple on the dance floor as the groom held his radiant bride close, whispered in her ear, and was answered by a sensuous swoon and mischievous laughter.

The officer spoke loud enough for Linda to hear. "It's beautiful, no? Of course, it's the love. When love fills the heart, the earth changes to heaven...but I'm sure I don't need to tell you two." The officer smiled at Linda and Tom.

"Oh," said Linda, "we're not married. We're traveling to the Amazon on business."

"Really," said the older woman at Linda's elbow, "how unusual, or maybe it's just American...so progressive. What is your business, may I ask?"

"Ahem," coughed Tom.

"I can't talk about it. I'm sorry," answered Linda.

"That's alright, I understand. Have you ever been to the Amazon before?"

"No, never."

"Neither of you?"

"No."

"Are you starting from Caracas? That's where I'm getting off to visit relatives."

"No, we're going to Lima, and from there, over the mountains."

"Then that's why we met," beamed the well-dressed woman. "How wonderful. Everything has a meaning, you know—everything is a sign of some kind. My husband, *Señor* Cliente, is the head of the Natural History Museum in Lima. You simply must visit him before you go on. He knows absolutely everything about the Amazon. He'll be happy to answer all your questions. How fortunate for you to have met me."

Tom touched Linda's hand. "Let's dance, shall we?"

She nodded and said, "Thank you," as they stood.

He walked her to the floor. They turned to the slow music. Tom pressed Linda closer. "The captain's right, you know. This is a perfect night to fall in love."

She pulled away. "I'm sorry," she said apologetically. "I need some air."

She stepped outside and stood at the rail in the moonlight, listening to the soft slapping of water against the ship's hull. The balmy tropical breeze blowing her soft chiffon wrap around her shoulders.

Tom approached her from behind until he stood almost touching her. "What's wrong, Darling?" he whispered, hands gently caressing her shoulders.

She faced him. "Tom, don't...please."

"Can I help it if I find you irresistible?"

"Yes, I'm not irresistible—lots of men have resisted me, most of them. Truman being the most recent and famous."

Tom's advance was slowed but not stopped. "Linda..." He leaned in, puppy eyed, angling for a kiss.

She twisted away. "I mean it Tom. When I agreed to let you come along, it was to be as partners, nothing more. This is business. I've sunk everything I own into this trip. Besides, you don't even know me, not really, you just want what you see, not to mention the fact that if Truman's alive, I'm still a married woman. And I don't want to be compromised."

Tom backed off. "You're right, of course. I know how important this trip is to you. The last thing I want is to get you mad at me."

"I hoped you'd understand."

"Come on back inside. Let's have a drink on it. Champagne cocktail?"

"No thanks. I'd like to stay out here alone for a while."

Rebuffed, his face fell. "As you wish," he offered, sliding out with a nod of the head.

"Thanks Tom, see you tomorrow."

Tom went back inside, leaving Linda alone at the rail.

She stood quietly looking out to sea, felt the gentle pitching of the deck, and watched the black distance swallow and release a band of stars at the horizon. Linda turned to the sound of laughter and saw the newlywed couple hugging and kissing in the shadows. She turned away.

"Love? Crap, who needs it?" She lifted her gaze to the night sky. "No distractions, right?" she asked the moon, hoping for a sign of some kind.

The night sky was clean and clear. A thousand stars littered the deep indigo surrounding the buttermilk moon. A shooting star streaked across the heavens, leaving a trail of fading sparks.

• • • ● • ● • • •

It was just after sundown when Sam pulled his canoe into the landing at the mission of La Merced. Mission Indians, lightly armed and standing guard beside protective torches, greeted him with warm smiles and soft words.

Through the crowd and shifting shadows came the almost comic figure of Father Julian, the ordained Benedictine monk. A short dark Spaniard with a hawk nose and a wide smile, he wore an old metal breastplate over his black robes and carried an ancient basket-hilt rapier.

"Yo, Padre!" hailed Sam, and the two men embraced with affection, then headed across the compound to a hundred-year-old collection of adobe buildings. As they walked, the sound of soft rhythmic drumming followed them.

"It's good to see you, my son."

"Looks like you're still holding your own."

"With the help of God and a few muskets. Come, let's eat."

"You got yourself quite an army here."

"All unnecessary but for that devil spawn, Snake Ghost."

"Snake Ghost? I thought we finished him."

"Gone for a while. Now he's back with a vengeance. He's even taken captives from the edge of the mission...young girls, mostly."

They entered a long, low, tile-roofed building.

The dining room was Spanish colonial—adobe, wood, and wrought iron—basic and unadorned.

Sam and the priest sat at the long dining table over simple fare.

"The country's become deadlier than ever."

"Gotta hand it to you for sticking it out."

"I don't have a choice, Sam. I'm here to dispense God's love unto victory."

"Love conquers all, heh, Padre?"

"Simply put, but yes, I believe so. The adversary can try to strip us of our sight, blind us, wound us, but the power of love can restore people's souls."

"I can't argue with you there. I just haven't had enough of it in my life to know. Well, I gotta get an early start, think I'll turn in."

They pushed away from the table. Standing, Sam fingered the bottle of wine. "Great eating, Padre—mind if I take this? Help me sleep."

"No, go on. Sure you won't stay for a few days? It's dangerous upriver."Sam took the bottle and headed for the door, where he passed a guitar hung on the wall. "No thanks, I gotta keep moving. Say, you ever learn to play this thing?"

Father Julian ran his hand lovingly across the smooth, polished wood. "No, try as I may, I seem only to be capable of the most unpleasing sounds. I've come to believe that fine music is the gift of a fine spirit, and not that of a rough country monk. I'm afraid I'll never hear it played well."

"Well, maybe God will send you a musical angel. Good night, Padre."

"Good night, Sam."

Sam walked alone into the night. Father Julian watched him go, then muttered a quiet prayer and crossed himself.

Sam sat on the edge of his bunk in the small room the friar had given him, one of several empty monk's cells that lined a wing attached to the chapel.

He was tired, tired of running, tired of standing still. He wondered if he had ever been happy and contented...maybe years ago, after he got home from the war, when he had been married to his high-school sweet-heart, before she had cheated on him and left him broken-hearted. Before he had consigned himself to the jungle. But that was ancient history.

What now? Who cares? He answered himself as he finished the bottle of wine, lying down, hoping not to dream.

His last impression was of the small statue of Mary, resting in a corner shrine, gazing down benevolently, arms open in invitation.

Chapter 8

Another two weeks at sea saw Tom and Linda passing through the canal at Panama, then heading south, along the western coast of South America, until finally they docked at Callao, the port closest to Lima Peru.

Linda readied herself in her cabin, excitedly looking out the porthole. There was so much to think about as she finished packing. The voyage had been agonizingly slow for her, largely because of Tom's presence, which inspired growing mixed feelings. She had accepted his offer to join her because she realized she might need assistance in some unanticipated situation. Besides, she didn't want to disappoint him by rejecting his offer to help—after all, he was her lawyer.

Now she questioned his presence, especially at night when he would try to corner her alone after a couple of drinks and get romantic. In a way, she couldn't blame him. He was probably getting lonely. After all, she hadn't given him any hint of what she had learned about Truman's treasure quest, so they couldn't very well discuss her plans. Now, all things considered, she could see trouble ahead with Tom, and was sorry she agreed to let him come along.

She sighed. *Nothing can be done about it now,* she thought, remembering that she had worked and traveled on the road for almost eight years, by bus, train and once by ship to France where she met Truman. All that had been in pursuit of work, or with dance troupes when she had earned her living as a chorus girl, a "hoofer" as they said—and she knew the signs.

Looking back, her life seemed to have been a tedious chronicle of successive wrestling matches with casting directors, stage directors, dance directors, leading men, hotel staff, admirers, and drunks. Drunks being the most honest about their intentions. Their approaches were sometimes different depending on their income or social status, but in the end, it was always the same. ..they wanted to use her to distribute their unwanted seed.

Men! she thought. *Not on this trip. Not until I'm rich, and maybe not even then, at least not until I can afford it.* It wasn't that she didn't like Tom, she did, but the chemistry just wasn't there, and she had no reason to indulge him. This trip was all about business and a struggle for her future.

Linda finished by slipping into a white linen dress made for the tropics, with a straw hat and lace-up white shoes with perforated toes and Cuban heels—then added a printed silk scarf while looking in the mirror.

She loved the newer art déco look. It had become popular a few years earlier, in the late twenties, with the discovery of King Tut's tomb. Now it seemed to have reached its zenith, and she had several favorite pieces. She chose a red and white bracelet with matching earrings.

The ship's horn hurried her to the deck, where she knew Tom would be waiting, insufferably punctual.

As always, Tom was immaculate in a white double-breasted suit, black and white spectators, and a straw optimal hat. He smiled when he saw her and said, somewhat predictably, "My, you look beautiful this morning."

Their luggage was brought up on deck, where swarthy porters helped them navigate the gangway to the line of people waiting to go through customs.

Once finished with the formalities of landing, they searched out a taxi for the seventeen-odd mile trip to the city itself.

• • • • • • • • • • •

The old car soon scaled the coastal bluffs, and took them through an unexpectedly dry countryside, past small roadside stalls and scattered houses, Lima's skyline growing closer by the mile. Linda had made reservations at a respectable hotel, and the taxi driver finally made his way through narrow cobble-stone streets toward the downtown, Plaza de Armas.

Linda became increasingly disappointed, as the clean fresh smell of the ocean was gradually replaced by the noxious odor of garbage rotting in the streets, a smell that even the perfumed scent of the jasmine, planted throughout the city, couldn't hide. Then there was the overall depressing sight of decaying colonial splendor in the dusty, yellow ocher Spanish facades.

The hotel sat just off the main plaza, past the central fountain and close to the cathedral, in the heart of the old city.

After haggling with the cabbie and unloading their luggage, they entered to face the front desk. The lobby was broad and open, with red tile floors and arched doorways that led into the dining room on one side and elevators on the other. Yellow and blue zig-zag tilework covered the walls, setting off the large potted palms that stood guard around the colonial furniture, furniture that was cushioned with Incan print material. It was picture-book Spanish tropical, but the heat and humidity followed them, despite the ceiling fans—so, their surroundings, which looked comfortable, weren't.

Linda felt slightly faint, envying, for a moment, the casual dress of those native women she saw wearing loose Indian garments and derby hats. The sea voyage had been a long one, and she had gotten used to the rolling motion of the ship and the cool air of the sea, now, on dry land she felt oddly uncomfortable and wanted to rest, so they agreed to separate and freshen up, and meet later.

Tom watched Linda cross the lobby to the elevators, where she disappeared behind closing doors with a smile and a wave. He waited for the arrow above the doors to show upward progress.

Satisfied that she wasn't returning, his expression became more business-like. He turned to the desk clerk.

"Where can I send a telegram?" he asked. The clerk pointed directions and Tom started off, thinking as he walked.

Things hadn't gone as he had wanted. He had tried to use his time with Linda to find out more about what she knew of Truman's whereabouts and what her exact plans were, even engage her in a romance, but she had acted distant, unreceptive. He wrote that off to her preoccupation with her wild-goose-chase. But her resistance was becoming annoying. Perhaps he had played it too compliant, too sophomorically romantic. Well, he could change that, become more authoritative—after all, she had responded to Truman and that was about his only good quality, that, and his money, of course.

Tom stopped at the counter that displayed newspapers and sundries. *What if something goes wrong? Something unexpected happens,* he wondered, his thoughts glancing over these questions as a pretty young attendant stepped to face him.

"I want to send a cablegram to the World Rubber head office in New York." He said, flashing her a knowing smile, watching her eyes sparkle as she smiled back and turned away for the paperwork.

This was all in keeping his options open—letting the chairman know of their progress without giving him any information that would undermine his own chances in any direction. It was a delicate game. Tom glanced around while the paperwork was prepared and caught his rippled reflection in a window. He smoothed his hair and straightened his tie, smiling at himself, imagining a life with Linda living in Truman's mansion, wealthy beyond his wildest dreams. Ironically, he also knew he could never really love her. Linda was unlettered and foolish, headstrong, and childish. He knew she would be an embarrassment in the affluent society to which he aspired—still, she might be the key to his future, so he had to play his cards carefully.

Tom felt a surge of confidence in his mastery of subterfuge, knowing he was superior in both intellect and cunning, not to mention his suave demeanor. Linda would come around.

• • • • • • • • • •

Linda found her room tired in its appointments, but with a lovely view of the plaza and its main bronze fountain.

She undressed, taking a few moments and a wet wash cloth to freshen up. The circulating air from the ceiling fan felt good as she sat on the bed and, withdrawing Truman's book from her purse, studied it for the hundredth time.

She was thankful that the book had been written in English. Even so, the narrative wandered through several centuries of Spanish exploration, starting with the conquistador, Pizarro. Although it was hard to understand, she found that if she followed the passages underlined in pencil, she could piece together a kind of lose geographic idea, a *best guess* of where the undiscovered Inca treasure city lay.

One thing that concerned her was that a page had been torn out of the back of the book. When checking the "Table of Contents", she suspected it to have been a map. *Truman must have taken it,* she thought, knowing she would have to content herself with a modern one. The trouble was that an original map would have been made before modern cartographers using scientific instruments had surveyed—and the original hand-drawn one might have used names and terrain features wrongly, meaning that applying old references to a modern map might be misleading.

None of that could be helped now. She just had to keep going.

• • • ● • ● • • •

They met around noon and followed Linda's itinerary to the river dock, where she expected to find the charter sea plane she had read about. Instead, when they approached the gate in the chain-link fence that separated them from a single-engine float plane, they were confronted by half a dozen stony-faced armed policemen. Tom smiled a bit nervously. "We want the owner of that plane, understand?"

The police eyed them silently as they raised their rifles.

The ride to the Lima Police Station was short, and soon, Tom and Linda, flanked by two unsmiling policemen, stood across the desk from a humorless and intimidating police captain.

The questioning went back and forth for what seemed like hours. "Once more," the captain said dully, tapping a pencil on his notebook.

"Please..." asserted Tom, "We're Americans, after all."

"Not you! Her!" he said angrily. "Now, *señora*, tell me again."

Linda was worn out from the heat and the repetitious questioning that only seemed geared to furthering their inconvenience. "We're trying to find the owner of that plane—to buy passage over the mountains—to find my missing husband," she pleaded.

"Where?" the policeman asked again.

"Look, if I knew where he was, he wouldn't be missing," she answered exasperatedly.

There was a long pause as the police captain looked over their papers again, then looked at her through narrow eyes.

"We're not allowing anyone into the backcountry. It's too dangerous. If you have no other business, I'll hold your papers until you get on the boat home."

The captain took their passports and threw them into a desk drawer.

Linda, outraged, leaned across the desk, a policeman close behind. "You can't do that!"

The policeman put a firm hand on her shoulder and pulled her back. The captain wore a deadpan expression. The silence that followed was broken only by a squeaky ceiling fan and the sound of muffled groans.

Tom got the message. They could do anything they wanted. "Yes, well, thank you very much for being so concerned about our safety...may we leave now?" he tried his best diplomatic tone.

The police captain shrugged. "I warn you. The pilot of that plane is suspected of smuggling. If we catch him, we'll shoot him, and anyone caught with him...understood?"

Tom took Linda by the arm and led her out. "No need to worry about us on that score. No need at all. We'll book passage tomorrow. Thank you so much...thank you."

Tom bowed and smiled his way out of the office, pulling Linda by the arm. She was angry but couldn't do anything but comply. The police watched them go, never changing expressions.

Once outside, they found shade under a close awning, away from the heat of the afternoon. Linda stood silently, arms crossed, angrily tapping her foot, trying to think of something else to do—maybe they should try to find the American Consulate.

Tom quickly assessed the facts. Their trip ending now could work to his advantage, giving him another few weeks on a sea voyage back to New York with Linda. More time to consider just how to tell her about Truman's letter, which he carried in a waterproof money-belt. By the time they would get to New York, he would be in a position to enforce Truman's will, and would depend on her gratitude and affection for a beneficial reward. If it didn't work out with her, he would have time to destroy the letter and reach an agreement with the company for a rewarding future. He just had to play for time and keep his options open.

"Well, we might as well go back to the hotel and pack. I'll fetch a cab," he said, stepping into the street and waving his arm.

Linda stood, lost in her downcast thoughts. She could see Tom wanted to give up. With no airplane, and walking out of the question, she didn't seem to have any way into the Amazon basin.

"This just can't be the end of the line," she speculated as she bit her thumbnail, "it just can't be."

A horse-drawn cab clopped to the curb. Tom opened the door and guided a distracted Linda aboard, then took a seat next to her.

"Take us to the hotel," he said. The driver nodded and laid a gentle strap on the horse's back, prompting it to lurch forward.

Linda suddenly remembered meeting Mrs. Cliente aboard their ship, and her suggestion that they meet her husband, an expert on the Amazon, before they ventured further.

"No," she said, suddenly hopeful, "take us to the museum before it closes."

Chapter 9

- -

The Natural History Museum was housed in a centuries old Spanish building, long-ago converted to that purpose. The dark and cool interior was lined with glass cases and shelves, all featuring exhibits related to Peruvian history.

They met *Señor* Cliente downstairs. He was an older man with thinning white hair and a wispy moustache. "I'm so happy to meet you," he said, taking Linda's hand and bowing slightly. "my wife cabled me all about your trip. Fortunately, we have an Amazon Hall upstairs. Would you like to see it?"

"Yes, please." said Linda, hoping against hope for some kind of answer, information, sign, clue-anything.

They mounted the stairs to the hollow sounds of school children's laughter echoing through the near empty building and were soon slightly jostled by a descending crowd of smiling students and their harried teacher.

The Amazonian Hall was cool and broad, with high ceilings. The usual shelves and glass exhibit cases were built of dark wood, and old paintings lined the walls on the left, while the right side was lined with tall windows, which admitted shafts of clear afternoon sunlight that highlighted the dust particles that filled the hazy atmosphere.

Set up in chronological order, the near end of the hall was devoted to the Amazon itself. Linda passed cases of stuffed animals and photographs of the jungles and rivers.

Cliente explained, "The jungle plays host to the most diverse ecosystem on the planet. The fauna is extreme. For instance, there are over two hundred varieties of snakes, most of them poisonous. And reptiles, several varieties, sixteen varieties of caimans alone, not to mention crocodiles."

Linda listened to the litany of dangerous animals, large and small, ants, spiders, mosquitos, panthers, and snakes, with rising concern.

"Who are those people?" she asked, pointing to a series of photographs.

"Ah," Cliente started, "Indians. There are many tribes still living in the jungle—headhunters mostly, some are rumored to still engage in cannibalism, but the practice is dying out with the spreading of the Church's message. Still, they are resistive of outsiders and the cycle of revenge wars is ongoing."

"It seems incredible." Linda said, thinking of the skyscrapers and automobile clogged streets of New York and the civilization she left behind in exchange for the dangerously primitive new world of the Amazon.

"Yes, the Amazon is not yet part of the modern world—it is full of strange people and places, and many strange things still happen there."

Tom was drawn to the photographs of the painted faces that seemed to stare back at him in defiance, then to a case of blow-guns and darts and bowls of poison, and another containing a series of photos showing the process the Indians used to shrink a human head.

My God, he thought, *this is worse than I imagined*. He found himself frozen, staring at the morbid end product—a shrunken human head, smoked black, lips and eyes sewn shut.

Suddenly, Tom felt a rush of something cold in his gut, and for the first time in his life felt a queasiness and the dry metallic taste of fear. Until now, this had all been academic. Tagging along with Linda on her little adventure, but not now. Tom felt he was seeing a warning. Those unsmiling faces glaring at him from black and white photos, with their war paint and unflinching eyes, were telling him to stay away. He suddenly realized that all he had ever done or knew wouldn't help him in that jungle. He would be effectively naked, living on the edge of a yawning, dark and utterly dangerous chasm that might attack and devour him at any moment. Linda had to be stopped.

So intent was fear's grip on him, he didn't notice Linda's interest shift to a large painting of a golden city, surrounded by jungle.

"What's that?" she asked, pointing at the illustration that glowed in the fading light.

"Ahh," said Cliente, "the famous lost city of El Dorado." His eyes shown with excitement and his voice rose as he looked up at the image, "The Spanish started exploring the Amazonian up-lands around fifteen-thirty. Pizarro had discovered the Inca of Peru and saw that they were awash with gold. They were so consumed with their greed for wealth that they ventured to find its source, here," he explained, touching a map in the mountainous area of Eastern Peru.

Linda tried to suppress her excitement. Cliente was pointing to the very area where she intended to search for Truman. The very area described in Truman's book.

"Did they ever find the city?" she asked, trying to maintain her composure.

"No," he continued, "some think it was all only a legend, a myth. Some believe there still may be a lost city somewhere, full of gold, guarded by Amazons, the woman warriors of the Inca."

"It all sounds like such a fairy tale," she said, gazing up at the painting, her tone filled with awe and hope.

"Well, you must remember, the ancient Inca stronghold of Machu Picchu was discovered only a few years ago. The territory is large and mostly unexplored, so anything is possible. There is danger, of course. Remember, a certain Colonel Fawcett disappeared in the Amazon about ten years ago, looking for the same city."

"What's that?" she asked, pointing at a small golden figure standing in a glass case, grinning at her, its hands upraised.

"Ah," said Cliente, "that's Inti, the sun god."

Linda recognized the statue at once. It was the same as the one she had found on Truman's desk. Her mind spun with possibilities. Before, in New York, everything had seemed so remote, impossible. But, standing here, surrounded by Spanish conquistador armor and weapons, Inca gold glittering from glassed-in cases, and hearing the stories told by Cliente, she understood why Truman had been so infected with a desire to find the lost city of El Dorado and its treasure.

Suddenly, her apprehension was gone. *This is the sign I've been looking for*, she thought, suddenly knowing she was on the right trail, feeling her determination reinforced with a vague sense of destiny. She stared at the painting, jaw flexing as she bit her thumbnail.

I'm going to do it, she thought. *I'm going to find what I'm looking for, and nothing's going to stop me.*

• • • ●• ● • •·

They returned to the hotel in silence. Tom's attempts at conversation went unanswered, and it annoyed him. He could see Linda was deep in thought and that worried him, too. She was still keeping something from him—what?

He had found the trip to the museum both frightful and enlightening. Reality had impressed itself on him. He had thrown a few camping clothes from Brooks Brothers into a suitcase and thought himself prepared. What had he been thinking? Well, it was over now. They would start back tomorrow—period.

They reached the hotel and, crossing the lobby, Tom tried to broach the subject. "Linda, surely you see everything is trying to tell you not to continue."

"What?" she answered distractedly.

"First the police, then the horror stories at the museum. Linda, be reasonable." He stopped and took hold of her arm, demanding her attention. "We don't have papers. There'll be no place to get money, no banks, no accommodations, only the most violently dangerous place on earth. Surely these facts must concern you!"

"Tom," she said, breaking his hold, "I don't want to talk about all that now—I want to think. Let's meet later for dinner, okay?"

She left him standing alone in the lobby as she strode to the elevator.

Once in her room, she sat heavily on the bed. Yes, Tom was right. Everything was against her, and she had every reason to quit and go home. Yet, yet, she knew she was on the right track. If only she had a break of some kind, she knew she would find the treasure she longed for, a treasure that would solve all her problems.

· · · ● · ● · · ·

The dining room was filled almost to capacity. Waiters in starched white jackets threaded their way through the tables of animated patrons as some couples danced to the Latin music that reminded Linda of Xavier Cugat, and she wondered briefly who had copied who. They were seated across from the bar, at a table close to the bank of French doors that opened out to the tiled patio, and the fragrance from potted flowers surrounded them as they ordered dinner.

What a beautiful place to be lost in, she thought, dreaming for a moment of sitting across the candle-lit table from some one...someone. She quickly dismissed her romantic fantasy as unwanted, but the thought lingered throughout dinner, and she found herself unable to enjoy the delicious shrimp cocktail she had ordered.

The after-dinner drinks found them sitting quietly. Linda had picked at her food and didn't feel like dancing. Conversation had been almost non-existent.

It worried Tom that he was being left out of her thinking, but he expected her to lament having run out of choices. The thing to do now was to gracefully turn her towards giving up and going home, but to stage the conversation in such a way that she would come to the decision on her own, or at least think she had.

Tom delicately brushed his mouth with his napkin, then shifted his eyes to her. "Come on, cheer up," he started, "let's face it. It's been a grand trip, but it may be the end of the trail." He patted her hand, bending his head to the straw in his drink glass.

Linda stared into her drink. She had to figure out how to continue. She was determined not to give up, especially not after seeing so many points of intersection between Truman's disappearance and the golden city of El Dorado. There still had to be some way....

"I'm afraid that without papers we haven't any choice," continued Tom, supplementing his argument, "Look, I know it's disappointing...but the company offer is still good. If we go back to New York, I'm sure we can try...."

Linda looked up and wrinkled her nose at something beyond Tom. "Trade places with me, will you?" She bit her thumbnail.

Tom looked around for the source of her annoyance. "Why, of course, why?"

"There're a couple of bums over there who keep staring at me."

"Well, they have good taste. I have the same problem."

"Tom, you promised.... Uh-oh, here they come."

Tom turned to see a seedy-looking American wearing a leather flying jacket and sunglasses, and his shifty-eyed Latin companion, making their way toward them. The two fumbled with chairs, then sat at the table, smiling drunkenly. The American spoke first. "Hi. I hear you're looking for me." A toothpick bobbed at the corner of his mouth.

Tom and Linda exchanged looks as the pilot shuddered, "J.J.'s the name, flying's the game. This here's Romeo, my co-pilot."

Romeo drooled a little through a red-faced smile and stuck out his hand. "*Mucho gusto.*"

No one shook, and his hand dropped to the table.

The pilot leaned forward. "I heard you wanna fly outta here. That true?"

Tom was suddenly alarmed. But Linda spoke before he could stop her.

"Yes, how did you know?" asked Linda, excitement bubbling in her voice.

"I'm afraid we have no visas," Tom interjected quickly, trying to forestall what he saw coming.

J.J.'s head swiveled from Linda to Tom. "We got a lot of friends on the force. Visas, no problem. Where do you want to go?"

"Somewhere on the Amazon," gushed Linda quietly.

"You got two hundred smackeroos, American?

"Yes—"

"That's pretty steep, isn't it?" groused Tom, trying to sideline the conversation.

"Hey pal, av-gas is up to twenty cents a gallon. Can you be ready at five a.m. with the cash?"

"Yes." Linda was smiling excitedly, almost bouncing in her chair.

"Where did you learn to fly?" Tom tried discrediting.

"Lafayette Escadrille. Would have made ace too if I hadn't kept cracking up...ahh, water under the bridge." J.J. grinned.

Romeo tapped J.J.'s arm. Both men looked to the bar where two uniformed policemen were showing photographs to the bartender. J.J. and Romeo slid out of their chairs and crept between tables towards the French doors.

J.J. gave a loud whistle over his shoulder, towards Linda and Tom. "O.K., no problem, five a.m., two C-notes...." He held up two fingers as they ducked out into the night.

Tom was incredulous. He could see his entire plan going sideways, destroyed before his eyes. Linda looked happily thoughtful.

"Good heavens, Linda, have you gone mad?" said Tom in a panicked attempt to correct things.

"What do you mean?"

"You can't trust those two? Not after meeting them and what the police said."

"I do, Tom, I have to, don't you see? It's a sign. It's our only chance." Her reassuring hand fell on top of his.

"Surely you wouldn't get into a plane with them, with all your money and no visa?"

"I didn't come this far to turn back now. Besides, I know those two look a little crazy, but once we get into the Amazon, everything will go as I planned. I'm sure of it."

"I don't like this at all, Linda."

She sat back, her expression hardening. "I'm going Tom. I'm going and nothing's going to stop me. If you don't want to come, then don't. Go back to New York. If you want to stop me, you'll have to call the police."

Tom quickly considered everything. He was trapped. "No, no, I'll see it through—it sounds dangerous down there. You'll be alone and might need me. I don't mind telling you I'm against it, that's all. But I'll go."

"Alright then," she said, smiling, new energy lifting her shoulders. "Let's get ready."

Chapter 10

----

5 a.m. found Tom and Linda waiting nervously on the corner, dressed in their new safari clothes, sitting on their luggage.

"I told you we couldn't trust them," said Tom, checking his watch. "They're already late."

"It's probably taking them time to sober up," she said hopefully.

They looked up at the faint screech of tires.

"Shhh, hear that?"

The sound of a car motor drew closer. Headlights rounded the far corner and raced toward them. A dilapidated touring car bumped up on the curb and skidded to a stop, almost running them over. J.J., grinning behind the wheel, was still drunk.

Romeo rode shotgun. He smiled over the door, waving a half-full bottle of tequila. "*Vamanos*!" he slurred.

"Hurry up!" encouraged J.J., reaching back to open the rear suicide door.

Tom and Linda shared a look of uncertainty.

"Come on, folks, we gotta be in the air by dawn."

"It's now or never, Tom," Linda said, standing and throwing her bags in the back, then jumping in. Tom paused, genuinely afraid. Realizing there was no other choice, climbed in next to her.

The touring car sped away, bouncing off the curb, the motor roaring as they raced erratically through the narrow, dark, cobble-stone streets. J.J. still shaking. Romeo, laughing crazily between drinks, turned and offered the bottle to the back seat where Tom and Linda were frozen, wide-eyed with fear.

J.J. turned off the headlights and engine and turned down a long wooden pier. The only sound was that of the tires bumping across the planks as they rolled to a stop behind a row of storage sheds. The grey light of dawn revealed three police guards, half asleep, warming themselves around a trash can fire behind the wire fence that served to guard J.J.'s silver float plane.

J.J. and Romeo quietly helped Linda and Tom with their bags, then J.J. put his finger to his lips and signaling silence, led them around the shed, away from the car and Romeo, to hide in the shadows behind a stack of crates.

"What's going on?" asked Linda, confused.

J.J. put his finger to his lips again and cut her off. "Shhh," he whispered as he signaled with his hand for them to stay hidden.

"Why do we have to be quiet?" she whispered.

"Not good to startle the police. They always start shooting. Shhh. Stay flexible."

BOOM! Linda and Tom screamed, as behind them, the tin shed exploded in a ball of fire. Romeo, grinning wildly, hair singed, chucked an empty gas can as he ran towards the gate, waving his arms and screaming. The police started shouting as they opened the gate and ran past them to the burning wreckage.

"Boarding time!" shouted J.J. as he grabbed Linda by the arm and started running for the plane, Tom and Romeo close behind.

They ran through the open gate and down a small duckboard causeway to the floating barge where the bobbing plane was tied. J.J. opened the side door under the wing and climbed in. Linda and Tom were half pulled, half pushed into the plane. Linda received Romeo's unwanted assistance from behind. His maniacal smile was made more horrifying by his pink eyes and smoking hair. Romeo threw most of the luggage in after them, then rushed to the front of the plane and set the engine crank.

Linda and Tom untangled themselves on the floor as J.J. banged on the controls.

"Damn, things never did work right." Then, "Contact!" He shouted out the window to Romeo who shouted back, "Contact!" and began turning the hand crank, forcing the engine to wheeze and whine to life, finally coughing blue exhaust flames and clouds of black smoke, as the propeller spun and police bullets started hitting the plane, sounding like hail on a tin roof.

Linda screamed as Romeo cast off the mooring line. Then, still laughing, he backed into the door, revolver in hand, banged away at the police, filling the cabin with gun-smoke and the smell of burnt cordite.

The plane gained speed, bouncing across the choppy water, as more holes were punched in the fuselage by angry sounding bullets. Romeo and J.J. laughing madly.

"I hope they left gas in it," J.J. yelled as he pushed the throttle ball forward and pulled back on the controls.

The plane bounced repeatedly, splashing water sounding hollow on the aluminum pontoons—then leaped into the air, barely missing a bridge. J.J. pulled hard back on the controls, and they entered a steep climb, throwing Tom and Linda to the rear of the cabin.

"Fasten your seat ropes," yelled Romeo, filling the plane with laughter.

• • • ● • ● • • •

The silver craft was dwarfed by the cloud covered snowy peak s... as it trailed a thin stream of white vapor.

Linda and Tom tried to compose themselves while J.J. and Romeo smiled at each other and passed the tequila. J.J. looked back into the cabin. "You got the money, right?"

"Y-yes."

"Well, hand her over." He stuck out a gloved hand.

"Not yet—not till we get there."

"Get where?"

"Cabo de Christos."

"What?" J.J. exclaimed, looking back into the cabin. "Look, lady, all you said was that you wanted to get somewhere in the Amazon."

"Yes, and that somewhere is Cabo de Christos." She bit her thumbnail.

"I've never heard—"

Linda screamed. Tom followed her look out the window and saw a large mountain outcropping rushing to meet them. Linda threw her hands over her face. J.J. threw the stick to the left, standing the plane on one wing, and banking it around the rock face—everyone sliding across the plane's interior.

Tom shouted, "Are you crazy? Pull up!"

"Can't. Too low on fuel. Must have taken a couple in the tank."

"What?!" they yelled in unison.

"We'll try for the plantation at Las Crusas. Should be about the end of our glide angle...probably..."

The plane descended the eastern, tree-covered mountain slope at a sharp angle, then leveled out as miles of rugged jungle began passing below, green to the horizon, lumpy with smaller mountain ranges, cut by ribbons of brown rivers snaking their way into the distance. The sight was hypnotic, which instantly brought Linda the realization of the vastness of the search area. Tom saw it too, hundreds, thousands of square miles of dangerous raw country, where they would be small as ants, unprotected and alone.

The engine choked and sputtered as the plane started losing altitude, whining dangerously. Linda and Tom were wide eyed as they white knuckled their seats.

"Are we going to make it?"

J.J. shrugged. "We'll either land or crash."

"Or both." Romeo shouted, waving his bottle with pink-eyed glee.

The plane continued its descent as it followed the dull brown ribbon of river, which wound through the unending umbrella of trees. Linda and Tom soon watched jungle foliage wiz past within inches of their wing tips. J.J. shuttered violently at the controls and Romeo had another drink.

They all heard a loud clattering and banging somewhere in the plane. J.J. turned to Romeo, "What the hell was that?"

Romeo shrugged. "Something must have broke," he said, waving his free hand.

"He's the greatest, ain't he? Hey, no problem. We made it," said J.J. as he turned around and smiled at Linda. "See! What'd I tell you? You gotta stay flexible."

The plane skimmed inches above the water through a dark tunnel of overhanging trees. The pontoons suddenly hit a rock and were torn away with a loud metal-ripping screech and a violent rocking of the plane. A wing tip caught a low limb and the plane ground looped, augering into the muddy bank with a splashing crunch. The propeller chewed into the weeds and soft wet earth as the plane settled and started to sink. Pandemonium reigned as, seized with panic, they scrambled over each other, trying to get through the cabin door and pull themselves from the wreck, finally splashing to shore as brown water swamped the broken fuselage.

They collected themselves on the muddy riverbank. Linda's fear turned to rage as she scraped mud from her expensive safari clothes. Tom was equally upset at having to shake the soggy filth from his hands. J.J. and Romeo seemed pretty happy.

"Not bad, huh?" announced J.J., smiling at them as they heard the plane sink further into the olive-green sludge with a bubbling gurgle.

"Not bad? You almost killed us!" cried Linda, trying to brush errant hair from her forehead with a muddy hand.

"Look at my clothes!" demanded Tom, spreading his arms to offer a better view of his mud-soaked new suit.

Linda surveyed the three men...yuck.

"Hey," said J.J. indignantly, "'Almost' only counts in hand grenades and horseshoes. Remember, any landing you can walk away from is a good one," he reminded them with a wink and a wag of his finger.

"In that case, this was an excellent landing, because I'm walking away from it right now!" Linda screamed, stamping her foot, splashing mud in all directions. Outraged, she turned on her heel and stalked away into the jungle.

"Hey! Where's she think she's going?"

"Linda?"

"Hey, Romeo, watch the plane."

Linda quickly found a river-side path and started to follow it toward a not-too-distant plantation house, indignantly brushing mud from herself while she huffed along with a determined gait. Tom and J.J. scrambled up the bank behind her.

"Hey, lady, you can't just walk around out here." J.J. said nervously, looking into the shadows of the close jungle.

She turned on them furiously, crossing her arms and stamping one foot. "I can do anything I want!" she said defiantly.

"Linda, what's gotten into you?" asked Tom, more than a little nervous.

"I'm sick and tired of being bullied, chased, given orders to, or shot at by every man I meet. This is MY expedition and I'm going to do things MY way. Look at my new boots! They're ruined!"

She turned again and headed towards the plantation house, waving her hand and calling out, "Yoo-hoo, yoo-hoo!"

The men gaggled behind her in a jittery silence. Tom became infected with J.J.'s open concern, rubbernecking the jungle. "Be careful, darling, might be dangerous..."

She entered the clearing at the edge of the house. "Non-sense—they're all out working or something, YOO-HOO!"

J.J. took hold of Tom's sleeve, then offered with a hoarse whisper, "Smells like Indians."

"Are you sure?"

"I know a thing or two about the locals."

SWISH-THUNK! A three-foot arrow flew past Tom's face to slam into a near tree.

"Like when to leave 'em be." J.J. turned and bolted back into the trees as Indians shouted, and arrows flew.

Linda was trapped in the clearing, turning from the house to the jungle and back again.

Tom wasn't sure whether to follow J.J. or Linda.

They both heard a shot and a man shout from the house. "Run for it, come on!"

Tom and Linda made a mad dash for the house as howling attackers stepped from the close brush, shooting arrows, blowing darts, and throwing spears.

Tom ran past Linda and sailed through the door first, crashing into the darkness beyond.

Linda faltered at the thresh-hold, stumbled, and was caught in Sam's left arm. For a breathless instant, they were locked together. He felt her breasts crushing against his chest—her arm, soft but strong, around his neck—her face, comically dirty—her eyes wide with fear, her lips slightly parted, and her breath smelling like hot candy. She looked up into his face—strong features, sun-burnt, nostrils flaring, his eyes riveting. She felt the corded muscles in his chest and his arms, squeezing her breath away.

"You, you're hurting me," Linda whispered hotly, putting a hand on his chest, not quite pushing.

He relaxed his grip, his fear of death suddenly overcome by his surprise at the thing in his arms.

Tom spoke, and the moment was lost. "You the owner here?"

"No," Sam said dryly, releasing her and looking outside, "they ate him a couple of days ago."

"Ate him?" Tom and Linda yelled in unison.

"I heard a plane. Can it fly?"

"No."

Sam fired another shot out the door. "Damn!" He turned to Linda—his eyes boring into hers. "Can you shoot?"

"Raised on a farm," she said, a bit shakily, brushing loose hair from her forehead.

Sam handed her his 30-40 Craig carbine. "If you see anything, shoot. Hell, if you don't see anything, shoot anyway!"

Then to Tom, "Come on, give me a hand." Sam led Tom to the back of the room, where a large antique hutch rested against the wall. The two men strained, pushing the heavy piece

of furniture. "Owner built an escape tunnel. Hid it with this -
then couldn't move it to get out."

Linda fired a shot out the door as they slid the massive china
closet, revealing a hole in the floor. Sam motioned them on.
Tom disappeared down the hole. Linda passed close to Sam, almost touching, handing him his rifle back. They shared a quick
questioning glance as she dropped into the tunnel. Sam looked
after her, scooped up his rucksack then followed, bringing up
the rear as fire arrows screamed in the windows.

Chapter 11

T om, Linda, and Sam splashed on hands and knees
      through the dark, rat-infested slime. They emerged from
a hidden entrance among twisted tree roots and glanced back to
see smoke rising from the not-to-distant farmhouse.

"Stay close!" whispered Sam as he took off fast and low. Tom
and Linda followed. Sam led them through the underbrush in a
frantic escape. Linda and Tom faltered. The sudden activity in
the heat and humidity felt like breathing through a wet towel.

"Mister...mister..." Linda said, gasping for breath.

Sam stopped and turned. "Call me Sam."

"Sam, can we rest a minute?"

Sam threw a nervous look at the back trail as Tom and Linda
gulped air.

"We can duck down. Surely, they won't see us," said Tom.

"They don't have to. They'll smell us."

"Smell us...like dogs?" Linda asked.

"Nope, better than dogs. They don't lose a scent in water. We've got to get out of here. Canoe's close, come on." Sam's urgency convinced them to redouble their efforts, and they stumbled ahead to the river that they could now hear.

They reached the river's edge and Sam's hidden canoe, stripped away the branches and broad leaves that covered it, and Sam quickly helped them aboard, Tom in front and Linda amidships. Then Sam pushed off and climbed in astern. He paddled with the current, steering the canoe through patches of sunlight and shadows, and away from the plantation.

Tom crouched in the bow and Linda sat quietly between them. Quiet until she realized she had forgotten her bag with Truman's book, "Go back to the plane," came her panicky demand.

Sam was incredulous. "What are you—crazy?"

"But I have to go back—please!" She pleaded, suddenly realizing that without Truman's book and the information she depended on, she would have to rely on her uncertain memory.

"We're not going back," Sam said with finality.

A quiet moment passed.

"Please, you don't understand. It's very important. I must go back—just for a minute."

Sam didn't even look at her.

"Good heavens, Linda," said Tom, happy to be putting space between them and certain death. "What could be so important?"

What could she say? She couldn't very well expose her source of information, not to a stranger, anyway. "I forgot my purse," she offered weakly, biting her thumbnail.

"Ohhh," Tom groaned, turning his back on her to look forward again.

Linda knew how stupid that sounded. Her head dropped in embarrassment, and she could feel her jaw flexing wildly.

Sam continued to paddle. When he felt the danger was past, he relaxed his efforts, and they drifted along with the current. "You can rest for a while," came Sam's voice, strong and low, "but stay quiet..."

· · · ●·●· · ·

The noon day sun was crackling hot, relentlessly beating down on their heads, arms, and neck. The air was still and thick with humidity and clouds of buzzing insects. Linda's blouse and safari jacket were soon drenched with perspiration and her legs felt cramped in the wooden canoe bottom, which took in just enough water to feel clammy.

Despite her personal discomfort and anxiety at the loss of Truman's book, Linda became enthralled with the beauty of the jungle. The jade green foliage was often broken by clumps of various colored flowers, and even more colorful birds sat among the branches or flew alone or in flocks, across her line of sight. The shrieks and calls of unseen wildlife accompanied all this.

Sam steered and watched his two new companions. *What the hell could they be doing down here?* he wondered. He couldn't imagine anyone less suited to the Amazon than these people. Now he was stuck with them, for a while anyway.

She looked back at Sam. He appeared every bit the disheveled hero. *What a strange person to meet way out here,* she thought.

He looked down and caught her eye. "What was all that about back there?" she asked, strangely wondering what her make-up looked like and wishing she had a mirror.

"Local politics...." he said in a disinterested tone, never taking his eyes off their surroundings.

Linda became increasingly frustrated at not knowing more, and Sam's silence gnawed at her. She thumped her fist on the canoe rail a few times, then almost bursting, she blurted, "I can't believe that the pilot ran out on us. What a coward. I hate cowards, don't you?" She looked back to Sam again.

Sam winced. "Yeah," he said dryly, the remark coming too close for comfort.

"You know, you haven't asked us who we are or where we're going?" she continued, trying to start a conversation.

Sam's eyes continued scanning their surroundings, alert for any danger. "Doesn't much matter," he said quietly.

Linda became even more desperate. The new events and surroundings, the unfamiliar jungle, and its animal sounds, exotic as they were, had her feeling uncomfortably alone and unprepared. She couldn't resist another try. "Have you ever heard of Cabo de Christos? It's somewhere on this river...it's where we're headed."

Sam took his time answering, "It's not on this river and it's not where we're headed..." his voice trailed off.

"What? Are you sure?"

"Of course, I'm sure. I just came up it, and there's nothing between here and Iquitos but three hundred miles of wild jungle, a couple of plantations and a mission, and that's where we're headed—Iquitos."

"You don't understand," she said, panic rising in her voice at the thought of all her objectives being thwarted, "I've got to get to Cabo de Christos, I've planned everything...I'll even pay you."

Sam continued paddling slowly, shaking his head, trying to conceive of the mind that could imagine this was some kind of guided river tour.

He finally tried to explain, "Lady, you're the one who doesn't understand. I'm going to Iquitos and I'm taking my little canoe here with me. So, if you want to get somewhere else on this river, find another way to get there. And as far as I know, there isn't any other way to get anywhere else—except walk, and I guarantee you don't want to try that."

Linda looked to Tom for help, but he offered none. He simply sat alone in a stupor of anxious confusion.

She settled back, frustrated and angry. "You're not a very friendly person—Sam."

"I'm not trying to be friendly, lady. I'm trying to stay alive—and keep you alive, too."

She turned away, unable to think. Everything was so unexpected, not at all what she had imagined, much less planned for, or arranged. This morning, she had been confident of success. Now she was a captive of circumstances well beyond her control, and her future thrown into doubt. Her hand wiped errant hair from her perspiration covered face. She leaned her elbow on the rail, her palm settling under her chin, fingers curled across her mouth.

• • • ● • ● ● • ••

Lengthening shadows signaled afternoon. The upper part of the jungle glowed yellow gold as it caught the dwindling light, standing in contrast to the lower part, which was now a study of dark blues and greens. A cloud of butterflies swept across the river, a porous mass of orange and black.

Sam still sat his position, unwavering, paddling, expressionless. Linda and Tom had fallen asleep, their heads nodding lazily against their chests.

Sam watched Linda. Her beauty was natural, child-like, yet she was very much a woman. He hadn't seen a skirt like her in...how long? He knew from the moment he saw her that in another time, another place, it would be easy to fall for her, given the chance. What guy wouldn't, but why bother? She wasn't there on account of him. Their meeting had been an accident. She was just a distraction, and distractions out here could be deadly—that meant that she was dangerous too, and he had to avoid her, avoid even thinking about her.

Linda stirred slowly, then woke with a start, and sat up, pushing the hair and sleep from her face. She smiled at Sam.

"Oh...how long have I slept?"

"Couple of hours..."

Tom woke behind her.

"Would you please pull over?" Linda asked.

"For?"

"Personal reasons, if you don't mind."

"If you have to go, go over the side." Sam nodding at the passing water.

"What?" she said indignantly. "Of all the..."

"Over the side or in your skivvies, but we're not pulling over, not yet anyway," he said, unmoved.

She had it. "Look, I don't care if this is your boat..." She stood, rocking the canoe; Tom grabbed the rails. "Of all the impossible men I've ever met," she yelled, "you take the cake, you big lunk!" She crossed her arms, her jaw flexing furiously.

"It's not safe," Sam said flatly.

"It looks safe over there." Tom commanded, pointed to shore and a small strip of sand.

Sam relented and angled for the small beach. "It's not safe. It's never safe and being with a crazy broad doesn't help."

Linda grunted and tipped her nose skyward.

Sam landed the boat. Tom took the bow as Linda, mustering all her dignity, headed for the concealment of some close brush.

Sam pointed to a closer place. "You better go over here where we can keep an eye on you."

She turned and gave him a blistering look. "Well, of all the..." then headed into the forest.

Sam started after her and was cut off by Tom, who was regaining his presence of mind, enough to want to assert control of the situation, at least where Linda was concerned. "Give her a moment, can't you? Surely you can try to be that civilized."

"You don't get it, do you? This jungle's a killer, twenty-four hours a day. It'll eat her alive, you too city-boy." Sam punctuated the comment by finger tapping Tom's chest.

Linda found a place of refuge behind a tree on a fallen log. Exhausted, she dropped to sit. Her head was spinning. The heat, humidity, and hunger had combined to weaken and disorient her. She hadn't eaten since the day before, and not much then. Now, after a chilling airplane disaster, an escape from head-hunters, and sitting cramped in a canoe under the blazing sun. She wanted to rest. To get a drink of water. She looked down and saw large red ants at her feet.

Sam and Tom stood on the shore, tempers rising.

"I'm only saying…" explained Tom, trying to convey command with his self-important, superior tone.

"Look, pal, I've been out here ten years, and you just got here. I'm not interested in anything you have to say about it."

They turned at the sound of Linda screaming, as she ran from the brush and ran for the river, tearing at her clothes. Sam grabbed her and ripped off her blouse. Linda slapped him, and still screaming, broke away and headed for the water, Sam running after her. Linda splashed, knee deep, into the river, screaming and brushing ants. Sam reached her, scooped her up and carried her back to shore, as behind them the water erupted with white froth and little silver fish.

"Piranha!" Sam cautioned as he dropped Linda and started tearing off her clothes and brushing her face. "Fire ants. If they get in her eyes, they'll blind her."

Linda soon lay in the soft wet bank, Sam rubbing her almost naked body with cooling mud. "This will help the stinging," she heard Sam say. She didn't know which was worse—her demand for privacy ending in her humiliation, or a strange man ripping off her clothes and seeing her half naked, or laying in the mud, having that same stranger smear her unclothed body with more slime?

Oh well, other men have seen me half naked, entire audiences of them. Besides, rich women on the upper eastside pay plenty for a mud-bath like this, and it does feel good. Oh, the hell with it, enjoy it. She had an impetuous thought. *I wish I had some cucumber slices for my eyes.*

Her sudden unexpected laugh seemed out of place.

• • • •• •• • ••

Night found them exhausted and dejected, sitting in uneasy silence around the small fire that crackled and popped, as it cast a sputtering orange firelight and dancing shadows. Sam had caught a small fish, and they had roasted it on a stick over the open flames. Now finished with eating, they each quietly contemplated the unknown future.

Linda wore clothes Sam had given her from his rucksack. She felt strange, his shirt and pants close to her body, worn thin and smooth from use and washing, frayed and patched, and smelling like him.

Sam checked them out, they were pathetic...what the hell, so was he. "Okay, here's the deal," he said, poking the fire with a small branch, "There's a slaving village a few miles down-river."

"We'll avoid it, of course." Said Tom.

"Can't. If we're lucky, we'll get some food and ammo."

"And if we're not...lucky?" asked Linda.

Sam shrugged, "End of trip."

"That doesn't sound like a very smart plan to me." said Tom, irritated and fearful at the same time.

"Yeah, well, it wasn't a very smart plan—you bringing your tenderfoot wife down here." More jabbing at the fire.

Linda entered matter-of-factly, "Oh, he didn't bring me. I brought him. This is my expedition, and Tom is my lawyer." Sam took a moment to digest that—then he grinned—then he laughed. Linda and Tom suddenly looked even more uncomfortable. "I've heard of people bringing some pretty useless stuff down here, but a mouthpiece's a new one."

Linda felt foolish and bit her thumbnail.

Tom said indignantly, "I'm a man too, you know."

Sam eyed him. "You sure better be, partner."

Linda allowed herself a little laugh. "He's right Tom, we must look pretty dumb."

Tom looked down. He didn't laugh.

"What the hell brought you down here, anyway?" asked Sam, letting his curiosity get the best of him.

Linda hesitated, not wanting to look more foolish, but finally relenting, "We're looking for my husband, Truman Dawson. He's been missing for over four months—"

"THE Truman Dawson, Mister World Rubber?" Sam interrupted.

"Yes, do you know him?"

"Nope, sure heard of him, though. You better not tell anyone else who you are."

"What, why not?"

"There's a war going on. The whole basin's up in arms. That's what you ran into when you landed. Slave against slaver...and World Rubber is the biggest slaver in the basin."

"I don't believe it. Tom?" She turned to him for an answer.

Tom, caught off guard, floundered, "Well, local managerial autonomy might...."

Sam finished, "The rubber business of the world is built on slave labor. Being Truman's wife, you just picked up about ten thousand enemies, most of them headhunters—a few cannibals, too. That has to be a one-day record."

They fell into another moment of thoughtful silence.

"What can we do?" Linda looked at Sam.

"Keep quiet—keep moving—try and get out alive...." he replied.

They all stared into the diminishing flames.

Chapter 12

The next morning, they pushed off early. Linda stopped Sam as they were boarding. "I, I want to apologize for the other day," she said, biting her lip.

"No reason to," he tried to let it go.

"I mean it. You were saving our lives, and I was being a brat." She stuck out her hand, "Friends?"

Sam looked at her, wishing she would continue being a brat—it made her easier to not like her. But looking into her apologetic eyes was disarming—she was so darn cute.

He took her hand. "Awww, forget it," he said, helping her into the canoe.

Once on the river, Linda tied her hair back with one of Sam's old bandannas. She had done some thinking, sitting around that quiet campfire. Sam was the key to getting out alive. That much was clear. She had been thrown off course, but her quest wasn't over by a long shot. It was just starting. The thing to do was to wait for another chance, another direction, and to learn about the jungle where she was marooned. She just had to think. She had been a Girl Scout, had camped in the forests surrounding her family farm, had been raised around animals, and not just domestic ones either, her woods were alive with snakes, deer, big cats, wolves, even large feral razor-back hogs. The thing was to not panic. After all, Sam wasn't panicked, even if he was a big lunk.

Tom sat in silence, absent-mindedly fidgeting with his clothes, trying to imagine how to gain better control of the situation. His background was one of wealth and education. He aspired to be among the highest rank socially and derided the lowest classes as necessary for serving the needs of those born to privilege. Here, he was out of his element and Sam's importance was obvious—but not to be confused with any sense of equality. After all, Sam seemed the sort of person one hired to do things, not to run them. That was his role as the superior person. The problem was that under their present conditions, Sam might assume an exaggerated importance, not in keeping with the rules of the more civilized society to which he and Linda would one day return. Sam's role in their survival might impress Linda out of all proportion, and he had to guard against that.

"Look!" She pointed to the shore. A crocodile slid off the muddy bank and into the river from under a large flowering shrub.

Sam couldn't help smiling at her. She was like a little kid on her first trip to the zoo.

"God, it is beautiful, isn't it?" she observed.

"I guess." Sam said, seeing the jungle with fresh eyes. It *was* beautiful. Maybe he had forgotten.

"Sam," she blurted, turning to face him, wide eyed and girlish. "If I fell overboard, and that crocodile tried to attack me, would you jump into the water and fight it with your knife to rescue me?"

He almost laughed at the thought. "Well, I'd probably try to shoot it first. You're not planning to jump in, are you?"

"No," she said, slightly disappointed.

They floated a little while. Sam had to ask. "Why would you think of such a thing?"

"Well," she said, "I saw a Tarzan movie as part of my research for this trip, and that's what Buster Crabbe did."

"A Tarzan movie?"

"Yes, you know, to learn something about the jungle and see how a girl might dress." She pointed again to the bank where a pair of colorful, parrot-like birds, suddenly startled, broke for the top branches.

Sam saw them as well. "Cotingas—there, a jacamar—" Linda looked to where Sam was pointing. A splash of color among the branches, "Hummingbird, sort of," he finished.

"I'll bet you know every animal in the jungle."

"Four legs and two—I used to catch them sometimes, for the zoos."

"Is that why you came down here?"

Sam thought—that was a lot of question, more than he wanted to think about right now. "Not really—gave me a reason to stay though," he answered without really answering.

"I thought you worked for the plantations?" queried Tom.

"Down here, you work for everybody sooner or later. I used to keep meat on their table. Bush hunter, guide, tracker for the army—anything short of slaving."

They fell quiet and drifted through jungle and time.

• • • ● ● • ● ● • • •

As more days passed, they fell into a predictable routine. Linda and Tom became more accustomed to their surroundings. Linda with farm-girl enthusiasm, Tom, not at all. He hated the inconvenience, and the physical conditions in general.

But most of all, he hated what he perceived to be a developing relationship between Sam and Linda. He could see that they had become friends, or at least friendly, smiling at each other as they seemed to want to bring a picnic-like attitude to this incredibly dangerous misadventure, not at all in keeping with the gravity of their situation. But there was nothing he could do about it—at least not yet.

• • • ● ● • ● ● • • •

The fourth morning, as they drifted lazily, they started hearing the drums. At first, the sound was mere reverberations, organic to the passing jungle, like the jungle's waking heartbeat. As time passed, the steady beating gradually dulled the senses with the relentless throbbing, almost hypnotic tempo.

"They're expecting us." Sam nodded toward the bank where they saw natives standing in the shadows, painted black and green and wearing feathered crowns, holding blowguns and spears. "Been watching us for hours. Well, I guess there're a few things you should know before we land. This camp can get pretty wild. Whatever happens, don't get excited unless I do. These guys all get high on chicha. Spook 'em and they can go crazy."

"What's chicha?"

"Local brew. If they offer you any, they're trying to be friendly, so just swallow and smile...."

Linda was nervous, Tom more so. The direct threat of death was new to him, and the building sense of terror felt prickly and cold. His skin was clammy, and his throat was dry and metallic tasting. He remembered those starkly ominous museum photographs of the headhunters—now real ones were staring at him out of the close brush.

His words came raspy, "I think we should make a run for it." His hands unsure of what to do grasped and released the canoe rails.

"Oh, Tom, can't you see? We're helpless," she said in a tone of resignation. "We have to do what Sam says. We have to trust him." She looked up at Sam, stoically paddling, "I trust him."

Sam felt her eyes on him and wished she hadn't said that. Someone trusting you was personal. It carried a lot of responsibility with it, and he wasn't sure he could live up to it.

• • • ● • ● • ● • •

The first indication of the slave camp was a battered bamboo dock and stockade at the river's edge. Gruesomely painted human skulls were decorated everywhere.

Sam landed the boat, and they all climbed aboard the dock as a group of wild looking Indians approached and surrounded them. The Indians smiled and pawed at Linda's hair, making her instantly uneasy at the attention.

"Blondes are a little scarce out here. Relax," Sam smiled and winked at Linda.

She tried to buck up, but her expression never quite made it. Tom was terrified. She could see him tremble as Indians stuck their grinning, painted faces close to his and plucked at his clothing.

Drums started pounding louder as an older white man wearing a dirty, thin-worn tropical suit pushed his way through the crowd. Von Vorhies flashed a lecherous, yellow-toothed smile. "Well, well...cheated death again, I see, eh, Sam?"

"Getting easier all the time, Jock."

Von Vorhies extended his hand to Linda. "Where are your manners, Sam? Aren't you going to introduce me to your charming traveling companion?"

He bowed and clicked the heels on his nearly worn-out shoes. "Joachim Von Vorhies, late of his Majesty's Hussars, at your service." He raised her hand to his lips, leaving an unwanted smear of saliva.

Linda was struck by his craggy face and his pale complexion, a deathly pallor that hinted at his hiding from daylight and reminding her of a creature she had seen in a vampire movie.

"Linda—" she started to say.

"And Tom, her husband." Sam said, cutting her off.

"*Welcommen*, my dear...and what brings you to us?" He placed an unwelcome arm around her shoulder.

"They want to build a summer place, looking for a little river property."

Von Vorhies' cold eyes narrowed above an oily smile. "That's my Sam, always the jokester. That's why we've always wanted to enjoy him for dinner."

"We're kind of in a hurry, Jock. Could I get you for a box of thirty-forty?"

Von Vorhies tipped his head toward Sam, still smiling. He licked his lips, lizard-like, "You out of ammo, Sam?"

Sam raised his rifle barrel, pointing it at Von Vorhies in a subtle move that only the two men noticed, but whose implication was clear.

"Not yet, Jock."

Von Vorhies grunted a laugh. "Very well, my friend, come on." Then to Linda and Tom, "Please excuse us. We don't get much of a chance to entertain outsiders very often, especially such lovely ones." His hand lifted her chin. She gulped, unnerved by his steady gaze and predatory smile. "Allow me to apologize in advance. You'll probably find our table manners a bit rusty. But please, make yourselves at home." Von Vorhies offered a deep bow and a sweeping arm. "*Mi casa es su casa*, such as it is."

"Come on, Jock, let's go." Sam nudged him with the business end of the rifle.

Sam and Von Vorhies walked to the small shack that served as office and store. Linda and Tom were left alone, surrounded by painted and feathered head-hunters. Linda sighed with acceptance and started strolling aimlessly. Tom, terrified, followed her. They passed cages of bound, sad looking captives.

"Good heavens, Linda. What are you doing?"

"You heard him, Tom...to have a look around. Relax, remember?"

They walked slowly, cautiously, followed closely by a crowd of curious natives who huddled behind them, talking among themselves, and picking at the western clothing.

In the trade hut, Sam worked quickly, jamming supplies into his open shirt front while holding his rifle on Von Vorhies. They watched Linda through the window as she ambled around the compound.

"Okay, Sam, down to business. How much do you want for her?" rasped Von Vorhies, his boney hand holding back the bamboo shade.

Sam said nothing as he took a can of gun powder off the shelf and stuck it in his back pocket.

Von Vorhies continued, "Come-on, put a price on her, anything—what's she worth to you?" He rubbed his hands together, eyes sparkling with unhealthy anticipation.

Sam looked again at Linda. She saw him and smiled from the yard, giving him a low wave.

How much is she worth? How much is she worth to me? He found himself afraid to really answer that question. "Forget it," was all he could say.

The German went on, almost frantically, "The entire country knows she's here. She's worth...my God, who knows how much? Besides, she doesn't have a chance and you know it."

"You talk like she's alone."

"That husband of hers," he grunted a contemptuously, "less than useless."

"I mean me, Jock."

Von Vorhies turned from the window to look directly at Sam. "You wouldn't stop an old friend from doing a little business, would you? Come on, I let you pass through a couple of weeks ago because the word was that you'd lost your nerve and on your way out." Von Vorhies peeked out the window again, ran his tongue over his lips, "Just think, you could get a little money to help with your...retirement. It's that or nothing, Sam, and I'll get her either way."

"I'm scared of lots of things, Jock. You're not one of them."

Von Vorhies tried to slide a knife from his waistband, but Sam shoved the rifle barrel under his chin, clicked the safety off with his thumb, his eyes becoming cold, deadly. "Try that again and I'll send you to hell! I mean it!"

Von Vorhies hissed through clenched teeth. "You're through on the river. You should have never come back. Give her to me and I'll see you get out alive. It's the best deal you can hope for."

Time dragged as their eyes locked in silent confrontation.

The sudden blast of conch horns and pounding drums arrested everyone's attention. Linda ran back to the shack, shouting, "Sam, Sam!"

Sam and Von Vorhies stepped out onto the small porch and into the fading afternoon light. Sam's rifle still pointing menacingly.

They saw that half a dozen war canoes had just landed at the dock, where painted Indians were unloading a new crop of slaves. A small party of newcomers walked to the trade shack, among them Snake Ghost and Soto.

Von Vorhies pushed the tip of Sam's rifle barrel away with his index finger and flashed a sinister smile. "Look, Sam, old friends. What a jolly little time we'll have tonight."

Linda and Tom were aghast at the unsavory collection of slavers and their hapless crying victims.

Soto saw Sam, his face darkened with hatred as he stalked directly towards him, eyes narrowed, and fists clenched.

"You know that man?" Linda asked, hoping the answer would be negative.

Sam shrugged, knowing that to shoot now would get them all massacred. "Sort of," he said. "I killed his brother."

WAP! Soto hit Sam full in the face, sending him to the ground unceremoniously.

Suddenly agitated, the Indians closed in around them, hooting and bobbing, weapons at the ready. Sam struggled to his feet.

Von Vorhies took Linda by the arm, leading her away like a Sunday stroll in the park, guiding the group across the yard to a giant thatched lodge.

"I'm sure you'll find this next presentation of indigenous culture very interesting, my dear," said Von Vorhies. "The natives are a very religious people…although, I admit, their theology can be a bit confusing…especially to newcomers. Forbearance, my dear, forbearance."

He bowed at the entrance of the lodge and swept his hand in a welcoming gesture that rekindled his almost forgotten memories of the imperial manners of a by-gone world.

Chapter 13

- -

T hey entered the huge lodge as twilight softened both light and shadows. Torches were lit both inside and out, and it took a moment to get used to the dark interior.

Linda gasped at what came into focus. At the far end of the room stood a large altar. An ancient cross hung with human bones and anaconda skin. Human skulls and shrunken heads hung from the rafters. Her stomach reacted to the stench of death.

Von Vorhies led Linda to a seat next to him at the head of the room. Tom and Sam were seated next to her. Soto, Snake Ghost, and his war party sat across from the fire. Indian guards stood all around.

Von Vorhies went on playing the part of the genial host, "You see, my dear, they live in a world of magic...spirits. And unlike us, they have the courage and innocence to live out their unique dreams, disturbing as some, less cosmopolitan people, might find them."

A native girl, Maria, about Linda's age, started to pass out bowls of foul-smelling liquid.

Linda turned to Sam with a weak smile. "Swallow and smile?"

"Yep," he said, his hand exploring his bruised jaw.

Linda smiled, raised the wooden cup to her mouth, her wrinkled nose commenting on the taste. Across the fire, Snake Ghost smiled his approval.

Maria made eye contact with Sam. A fleeting look that hinted at some yet untold message.

Von Vorhies went on, "Now, ladies and gentlemen, please excuse me while I try to conduct a little business." He shrugged, "Life goes on after all." He turned to Soto and asked, "*Cuánta para la rubia?*"

All eyes across the fire shifted to Linda.

Soto exclaimed, "*Cinquenta mujeres.*" A large murmur went through the crowd. "*Y diez mas por mi enemigo.*" He spit in Sam's direction. "*Yo querro mata él.*" He drew a finger across his throat. His grin was dark and dangerous.

"What's going on?" asked Tom.

"He's selling us," answered Sam, rolling his shoulders and clenching and unclenching his fists.

"What!" Tom and Linda replied together.

"But, but that's not legal," Tom said authoritatively.

"It's not RIGHT to sell people," implored Linda.

"*Vale.*" The German nodded his acceptance, then turned to them. "In some quarters, you both may be correct. Here, however, it's quite acceptable, I assure you."

Soto, red-eyed, fists clenched, came around the fire at Sam, advancing right across Tom, who raised his arms in self-defense and asked, "Can't we settle this without violence?"

"No, I don't think so." Von Vorhies shook his head.

"What's he going to do now?" cried Linda.

"He's going to try to kill me," replied Sam, taking Soto's kick, and sprawling into the darkness, canned goods rattling out of his shirt.

Linda clutched Tom's shoulder, shaking him. "Help him, do something!"

"You mean physically?" he gulped in a horrified tone.

Soto followed Sam. Sam rolled on his back, shot his feet up into Soto's groin. Soto sagged and groaned.

Sam got up, raising two clenched fists, "Okay, pal, come on!" The two men crashed together, trading body numbing, bone cracking blows.

Tom winced at the sounds, while Linda cheered Sam.

Soto went down close to the fire. On the rise, he threw a handful of hot ashes in Sam's face. Sam's hands went to his eyes, and Soto launched a powerful kick to his groin. Sam doubled over with a groan. Soto smashed a vicious double-fisted blow to the back of Sam's head. Sam sagged, going down to one knee.

Linda jumped to her feet, throwing herself at Soto, shouting, "That's not fair! That's not fair!"

The Indians cheered, Snake Ghost most of all. Soto tossed Linda away with an angry shrug, like a bear shaking off a small hound. Then he turned to the crowd and, sporting a bloody smile, he raised his massive arms and bellowed his victory like a mad bull.

Linda, coming out of nowhere, swung a right roundhouse that whistled through the air, and hit the big man square on the nose with a wet sounding SMACK. Blood spurted and Soto dropped to the seat of his pants with a dusty thud.

A thick silence crackled electrically through the lodge.

"My God, Linda," gasped Tom.

The expression on Soto's face darkened from disbelief to pure hatred. He pulled himself up slowly, growling with anger, muscles tightening and chest heaving, until he towered over her. Linda, outweighed by two hundred ugly pounds, stood her ground, her jaw flexing like crazy, tears of fear welling in her eyes, her fists trembling in front of her.

"C-come on you, b-big bully!" she stuttered, blowing a lock of hair from her forehead.

Sam, Tom, Von Vorhies, Snake Ghost, the Indians—everyone was instantly filled with awe.

Soto threw up his arms and bellowed his rage. Snake Ghost spoke quiet words and Indian spears were leveled. Soto froze.

The hut went quiet as everyone watched dumbfounded.

Snake Ghost stood and stepped to Linda, smiled and offered her his bowl of chicha, pronouncing to the crowd, "*Ella tiene una corazon muy fuerte, como guierro.*"

Bewildered, Linda looked to Von Vorhies.

"It seems you have impressed the venerable Snake Ghost himself. He says you have the heart of a warrior, a very great compliment indeed," he nodded solemnly. "He's offered you his chicha out of respect."

Linda smiled back at Snake Ghost, "Smile and swallow?" she asked Sam, now dragging himself to a sitting position.

He nodded, "Uh-huh," as his hands explored his battered ribs.

Linda took the wooden bowl, sipped the foul-smelling liquid, shuttered at the taste, but managed a smile.

Snake Ghost beamed, baring his teeth, filed to sharp points, and painted black, then took Linda's hand and held it aloft. She grinned and winked at Sam as Snake Ghost spoke, "*Quiero comerme el corazon de ella para tomar este poder!*"

Snake Ghost continued to smile as Von Vorhies translated, "And to honor you, my dear, he's going to eat your heart to gain that power."

"What?!" exclaimed Linda, her expression fading, as painted warriors closed in around her.

• • • •• • •• • • •

Drums pounded and flames leapt into the jungle night as head-hunters danced around a campfire, or shouted war songs and drank their narcotic brew by the gourd full.

Linda, Tom, and Sam watched the proceedings from inside their bamboo cage, knowing that when the sun rose and the festivities stopped, they would meet the agonizing fate being prepared for them.

Linda sat depressed and dispirited. Yet, even resigned to death, she was surprisingly calm. Her thoughts went to how her headstrong and foolish insistence on following Truman had resulted in them all having to suffer the ultimate price. Their doom was sealed, and she was profoundly sorry, especially realizing she was powerless to prevent it.

Sam, as always, was stoic. More angry than afraid, he waited and watched for any opportunity that might develop for escape. He'd been in tight spots before, usually the result of his bravado and lack of self-concern. He couldn't blame anyone else. It wasn't Linda's fault, or Tom's, it was just one of those things—fate, luck, or curi-puri, who could say? His false courage had already been crushed out of him on that mountain of death. Now he just sat and watched, determined not to give up.

Tom was a different story. He felt like an innocent bystander who'd been thrown into a terrible accident against his will. Now he was going to die because of someone else's stupidity. He quaked with fear. His knees were drawn up and his arms were locked around his legs. He trembled uncontrollably, knowing that if he released his hold on himself, he would simply fall to pieces.

They sat in their own world of thoughts as the shouting and drumming went on for hours, becoming louder and more violent as the moon rose and the screaming warriors became gripped by the hallucinogenic effects of the chicha

"Ohhh, this is all my fault," said Linda. "I know it's too late, but I want to tell you both how very sorry I am for getting us all into this."

Moments of awkward silence between them followed.

"That husband of yours must be quite a guy," Sam ventured, still intent on their surroundings.

"Truman? Oh, I don't know. I don't even care about him anymore, not really," she sighed, her gaze shifting from the dirt around her feet to Sam's questioning eyes.

"Then I don't get it. Why are you down here?"

Linda thought, *why not tell them, what good would any secrecy do now?*

"My husband's missing, that's true, but I'm not after him. I was after what he's after." She looked away again.

Her confession aroused Tom's interest. "What are you talking about? You said you knew where Truman was."

Linda bit her thumbnail, then continued glumly, "I know. It's so confusing. I found an old book of his and I realized he was on the trail of Inca treasure when he disappeared."

"So, you're following some old Spanish paper back treasure story?" asked Sam, his disbelief palpable.

"Oh, Linda," groaned Tom, "Why didn't you tell me?"

"I figured if I followed the same trail, I'd find Truman or the treasure. Either way, I'd have enough money to survive, maybe even get rich," she shrugged.

Sam shook his head. "You should have figured, if you followed the same trail, you'd end up the same way—missing."

"Yes, I should have. I didn't. I'm sorry." She sighed, pushing dirt around with her feet.

The flames and shouting grew louder, the frenzied drumming reached a crescendo as the fearsome warriors screamed and shook their weapons, dancing to exhaustion.

Sam noticed Maria standing close, and when their eyes met, she seemed to make a small signal with her hand, then quickly moved past.

• • • ● • ● ● • •

Dawn broke across the river, cool and cloudless.

Sam, Linda, and Tom still sat quietly in their bamboo cage. The camp began stirring to life. Indians roused, still groggy from the previous night's revelries. Some started stoking the large central cook fire. Drums sounded again. Tom licked his lips, his hands wringing the bamboo bars. Linda looked defeated. Sam eyed the camp for any chance of escape.

Tom, agitated, burst, "Damn! We can't just sit here. We have to do something."

But Sam saw Maria again, holding a brick-sized bundle, hovering close. "Wait," he said hopefully, motioning with his hand for everyone to pause.

"Wait? Wait for what, the chef?" Tom cried.

"What are you thinking, what's going on?" asked Linda, searching the camp for some reason for Sam's optimistic tone.

"I have to talk to someone," continued Tom, "Convince them we're worth more to them alive than dead. Negotiate some sort of compromise."

"Forget it, Tom, this isn't Wall Street," Linda responded.

"Maybe not," he snapped, "but Von Vorhies is a businessman, and a businessman is a businessman the world over. I understand them, we speak the same language."

Linda shook her head, "Oh, Tom..."

"Well, here comes your chance." Sam pointed to Von Vorhies and Soto coming toward them, leading a large party of painted head-hunters. The war party reached the cage, and the natives leveled their spears as they opened the bamboo door.

Linda gave a small sigh as she turned, gently looked into Sam's eyes, and whispered, "Goodbye, Sam."

Sam touched her cheek, saying softly, "Hang on, darlin', it's not over, till it's over."

Linda was dragged out. Tom made a desperate grab for Von Vorhies sleeve, shouting, "Wait, wait! Von Vorhies, listen. Whatever you're being paid for us, I'll double it, triple it, if you set us free."

Intrigued, Von Vorhies raised his hand, suspending activities. "Cash?"

"Well, some form of negotiable paper—"

"Any discount rate?"

"Local or foreign bank?"

Von Vorhies considered for a moment, rubbing the stubble on his chin. "An interesting offer, but under the circumstances, I'm afraid too impractical to entertain." Then to Linda, "I'm sorry, my dear. I really am, but you must understand, there's nothing personal in this. It's only business."

Linda regarded Tom, "You're right Tom, same language."

With a shout from Snake Ghost, the party started dragging Linda toward the fire. When all the attention in the camp was on Linda, Maria slipped her bundle through the bars to Sam. Sam opened the bundle to find his knife and pistol, then quickly explained his idea to Tom.

Linda was dragged between Von Vorhies and Soto, surrounded by painted warriors. Snake Ghost chanted and danced around the fire.

Von Vorhies, waxing eloquent, said, "Try to be philosophical about it, my dear. Snake Ghost is trying to do you a great honor. Why, you'll live on in myth and legend long after we're all gone. Look, he's even ordered all the women of the camp to make extra chicha for the occasion."

Linda followed his gaze to the line of native women, sitting on the ground, chewing leaves, then spitting the masticated liquid into gourds. She stopped dead in her tracks, shaking loose of her guards.

"Wait!" Linda yelled, holding up her hands.

Everyone froze, as suddenly outraged, she turned on Von Vorhies, stabbing him in the chest with her finger, yelling at the top of her lungs, "That's chicha? That's chicha? They're spitting into the freaking gourds! You let me drink that crap?"

She pushed him away hard and started gagging and spitting, arms flailing the air. Everyone stood back in surprise. Snake Ghost stopped dancing and started smiling, shouting words of encouragement to her.

"Oh, oh, I drank their spit?! I drank their spit! She choked and gagged, Oh you, you...."

Soto, with a growl, grabbed and shook her like a rag doll. BLAM! A shot rang out. Soto stopped as the top of his head exploded into a cloud of pink haze. Linda and Soto stared at each other. A trickle of blood oozed down his forehead, and he fell over dead.

More gunshots, and the camp broke into pandemonium as Sam, pistol in hand, rushed to Linda. "Come on!" he yelled, throwing his can of gunpowder into the fire as Tom and Maria snatched Sam's rifle from the trade hut. Sam grabbed Linda's arm—fired a couple of shots into the screaming mass of howl-ing head-hunters, but Linda tore herself free, shouting angri-ly, "Swallow and smile?! Swallow and smile?! What the hell's wrong with you?"

Indians whooped arrows whizzed by. Sam pleaded in desper-ation. "Let's talk about this later—please?"

Linda, too mad to care, crossed her arms defiantly, give him an icy stare, her foot tapping angrily, her jaw flexing like crazy.

With one quick motion, Sam bent down, grabbed her around the knees and lifted her over his shoulder, then ran for the canoe where Tom and Maria were nervously waiting. On the run, Sam continued dodging arrows and shooting at attackers, while an angry Linda bounced on his shoulder.

"How could you?!" she shouted, her fists beating his back-side.

Sam fired another shot on the run. "I'm sorry, okay?"

BOOM! Sam's can of gunpowder exploded in the campfire, scattering the regrouping Indians.

Sam bundled Linda into the canoe as she continued to gag, and with a few strong strokes, they were midstream.

Sam, Tom, and Maria paddled furiously, while behind them, three long war canoes full of howling braves, hove into view. Linda pulled her head up from the far side of the boat, looking pale and drained.

"You okay?" shouted Sam.

Exhausted, she nodded.

"Then paddle or shoot!"

Linda snatched up Sam's carbine from the bottom of the canoe and aimed back at the pursuing war party. Snake Ghost,

standing in the bow of the lead canoe, screamed blood thirsty
war cries, while his braves loosed arrows and spears.

Paddling as hard as they could, they were still no match for the
experienced native rowers. The distance between the two parties
splashed closer and closer as paddles drove the canoes faster.

Linda, trying to pick a target in the boats behind them, swung
the rifle barrel back and forth, each time crossing in front of
Sam's face. He ducked and paddled, "Hey, watch it with that
thing!" he shouted, then flinched as she fired a shot close to his
head, peeling a warrior out of a canoe.

She continued to work the bolt, yelling, "Eat MY heart, will
you?! Screw you!" BLAM! Another shot went off past Sam's
head and another brave fell...then another.

They paddled through the quickening current. Linda fired
again and Snake Ghost's canoe smashed into a large boul-
der—the white water sweeping away an angry crew. As Linda
looked on, the two remaining chase canoes started to slow and
pull to shore.

"Sam, I think we won. They're giving up."

"No, they're not. They just don't want to shoot the falls."

"Shoot the falls?!" Linda screamed, looking around, realizing
that the large encroaching boulders studding the narrowing
passage were causing the river to quicken its flow.

The canoe was driven forward, dangerously out of control,
as tumultuous churning water drenched them. Ahead, raging
white water boiled up into white mist, as the roar of the cascad-
ing falls grew deafening.

Everyone screamed. Linda looked at Sam. He was screaming
too but smiling as well. She got it—it was like the first time she

jumped from a barn loft into a waiting hay wagon, not knowing if she would make it or not. It was like a crazy roller-coaster thrill ride at Coney Island. She half turned and threw herself into Sam's chest as they braced their legs against the canoe's sides. Sam wrapped his arms around her, squeezing her tightly as her head pressed against his shoulder, both laughing and screaming, giddy with fear and excitement.

The waterfall, perilously high and surging fast, flung the canoe out into space with all hands shrieking. They felt a moment of sickening weightlessness as the churning water below rushed up to meet them.

Chapter 14

S am, Tom, Linda, and Maria struggled to help each other make shore—while coughing and spitting, they crawled to cover. Finally, wet, exhausted, and gulping for air, they collapsed in the shadows among the roots of a riverside tree.

After a few moments, still out of breath, Sam and Linda shared a look. Their hands reached out and found each other's, their fingers intertwined, squeezed, and giddy with the thrill of survival, they began laughing.

Slowly at first, then building hysterically, befuddling Tom, bewildering Maria, and expressing something deeper, something that they both felt, but didn't dare admit.

• • • ● •● ● ● • •

Later, when they had reassembled their composure, they all sat together, assessing their condition.

"Snake Ghost..." Linda said proudly, "I think I got him."

"They'll look for him. Bury him, maybe eat him," Sam shrugged, "Then they'll come after us... we have a few hours, days maybe."

"We lost the rifle...the canoe...now what?"

"I still have my knife." Sam patted the scabbard on his belt. "But going overland is too slow, too dangerous. They'll be watching the river, too."

"Not for Indians," smiled Maria.

Maria's English surprised Linda and Tom.

"This is Maria. She rescued us." Sam took Maria's hand and kissed it, bringing a shy smile to her face. "I mission girl," she said proudly. Linda shook her hand, "Hi, Maria. Thanks. I'm Linda. What were you saying about Indians?"

Maria continued, "We dress like Indians...build raft...get to mission...maybe."

"It'll never work," said Tom.

"Got any better ideas?" asked Sam.

Linda fingered her torn shirt. "Sounds like a great idea to me. I could use a new outfit," she said, hoping to sound enthusiastic as she exchanged smiles with Maria.

Sam was quick to try and implement the new plan. "Okay then. Tom, you and I'll look for some balsa. Linda, you help Maria with the disguises. We better get out of here as soon as we can, okay?" He surveyed the surrounding faces for other ideas. Only Tom looked reticent with downcast eyes but offered no objection. "Okay then!" Sam said with a smile, "Let's get going."

In the jungle, Sam seemed energized by their new lease on life, but Tom looked haggard and withdrawn as they huffed and strained, pushed and pulled and tore balsa saplings out of the earth.

Half a day gone, Sam and Tom carried their raft poles into camp and found Linda and Maria working together like old friends, laughing and talking quietly. Sam squatted by them, looking at their handiwork—large leaves filled with colored substances and lengths of raffia.

"How's it going?" he asked.

"Fine," Linda nodded, "We have ash and berry juice for dye, oh, and grease... we'll use that on our hair. Grass for skirts...and seeds to make jewelry."

Sam smiled at Linda. She started to smile back but faltered and turned away. Sam wondered if the connection he thought they had, wasn't there. *Don't be a dope*, he said to himself, turning away from her.

Tom watched them. Something had changed him in that slave village, something inside of him. He couldn't stop shaking. He could see himself tremble and felt that part of him was out of control. It made him jittery, angry.

He didn't like being overshadowed, and something in their smiles made him jealous. It made him angry that he should feel jealous of this backwoods Neanderthal. They were acting like everything was just inconvenient. No! Things weren't just inconvenient, they were deadly. Didn't they realize? They were just going along as if tomorrow they'd wake up in New York. Fools. They were blind fools. Worse, it seemed Linda was becoming infatuated with him. Didn't she realize he was a dead-end loser, no matter how brilliantly he shone in these primitive circumstances? Tom saw danger in their growing relationship and knew he had to interrupt their attraction before it went any further. He had to find a way. But more than any of that, he had to stay alive.

"She good worker." Maria nodded.

"Well, we better get back to work, too. Hey, you hungry?" said Sam.

"Yes!" came the universal reply.

"Good. I saw some tracks back there. Maybe I can find us a—"

Linda cut him off. "Stop! Kill it. Cook it. Feed it to me, but don't tell me what it is."

"Fair enough. Come on, Tom."

"Oh, go ahead. I don't seem to be much good at this Tarzan business."

They all felt uncomfortable with Tom's attitude. Sam offered him a smile; and, getting no response, headed into the jungle.

When Sam had disappeared, Tom turned to Linda, "Seems like everyone is enjoying this little adventure but me."

Tom's eyes pleaded with Linda for sympathy, but Linda only looked down at her handiwork. She was too busy helping Maria and thinking of other things. She thought about the times she had helped prepare costumes back-stage in small theaters, laughing to herself at the idea of how she was now making costumes for an escape act.

Linda thought about Sam, too. What would have happened to her without him? But as much as she wanted to give in to the attraction she was feeling, she reminded herself that she mustn't. She wouldn't let herself. She couldn't. She couldn't afford to fall in love with him. It would ruin everything. They could be friends. They *were* friends—sort of—but that was all. That was all it could be, ever.

No distractions. Remember?

• • • ● • ● • • •

The next day was spent getting ready. They had dried the balsa the best they could over slow burning fires, then lashed them together with twisted vines. They bundled their extra possessions in the clothing they weren't wearing and tied the bundles to the raft. They accumulated such food as they could, including meat that Sam had jerked over a slow fire.

On the third morning, they prepared to leave. Sam's hand scooped cold ashes from the dead campfire and mixed them with grease rendered from cooking a small pig. Sam and Tom, skin tanned with berry juice, wore the remains of their tattered clothing to resemble mestizo river rats. Sam laughed as he darkened Tom's hair with a combination of ashes and grease. "This is so nuts, it just might work."

Tom wasn't amused. He held up what was left of his now dirty and torn coat. "This jacket cost twenty-five dollars at Brooks Brothers," he groused. "This idea won't work, and you know it."

"You better hope you're wrong," said Sam, then turned toward the bushes that served as a dressing room for the women. He called out, "How's it going in there?"

They heard Maria giggle.

Then came Linda's voice, "Almost ready."

They saw movement in the leaves. With the flash of a smile, Linda, Maria following her, stepped into the camp. Sam and Tom were too shocked for words.

Linda had undergone a tremendous transformation. Her once blond wavy hair was now black, straight, and decorated with flowers. Her skin was dyed a buttery bronze, and her body was only slightly covered by a skimpy native grass skirt. Her breasts were clearly visible under strands of seed jewelry. She smiled and did a little stage bow, one foot behind the other, her hands spread at her sides, her head lowered, she said, "Ta-da." Then she looked up and smiled coyly.

Maria giggled. "Well," Linda said, crossing between the two mesmerized men, "Let's get going."

• • • ● • ● • • ••

An hour later, two mestizo traders and two native girls rafted down the river. Sam stood aft, poling. Tom sat astern at Sam's feet. Maria knelt at the bow on watch, and Linda lay stretched out in the sun amidship.

"My God, what a gorgeous day," she said, holding her hand up to block the sun from her eyes.

"Is that all you can think about?" asked Tom, a bit sullenly.

"That's all I want to think about." She glanced up at Sam. "How about you, Sam? What are you thinking about?"

All eyes looked at him, but he said nothing. Trying not to stare at Linda, he just grunted a laugh.

Linda closed her eyes and Maria giggled.

Linda knew it was unfair to flaunt herself, openly parading her nudity. She had done it many times before from a stage and knew the effects. Well, she was no nun, so why pretend? The time she had spent with Maria had been very profitable. She had learned the Indian woman's way of dealing with a woman's issues in the jungle. That had been very helpful, and nothing found in a travel book. And about the nudity—Maria told her that nudity was common and natural. So, that's how she would play it—natural. It would be hard on her too, drawing uncomfortable looks from both Tom and Sam, but if Maria could act unaffected, she had to also, and the boys would just have to get used to it. Maybe when they did, they would stop ogling her.

"How long before we reach the mission?" asked Tom?

"Three - four weeks," came Sam's answer.

They poled through a large trailing barge of yellow water lilies and under hanging bowers of colorful, sweet-smelling orchids.

· · · ● ● · ● ● · ·

Everyone was thankful for Maria's presence. She brought a lot of jungle knowledge—things Sam had never heard of. She made a potion from the sap of a tree that, when mixed with the dye they wore, helped keep away the buzzing clouds of flying insects. Another potion relieved the stinging of small bites, and still another removed hair from arms and legs, places the Indians kept bare to discourage accumulating the small critters who would take up residence in warm patches of hair or fur.

Whenever they stopped, Sam would cut bamboo spears, sharpen the ends, and harden them in the nightly campfire.

He used them to bring down small game, or wading into shallow water, close to the sheltering rocks where little whirlpools formed to catch fish.

As the days wore on, more and more, the afternoon rains began to pick up. At first, little squalls that sprinkled. Later, they sometimes turned unexpectedly heavy, necessitating that the company seek shelter earlier than they wanted, soon finding their travel time cut in half daily.

One afternoon, as they rounded a bend in the river, Maria warned, "*Señor*!" pointing to the sky ahead.

"Yeah, I see it," Sam said quietly.

Everyone looked at the trail of smoke on the horizon that drifted up from the tree line.

"The mission?" asked Linda.

"No, too close. It's another plantation."

"What will we do?"

"Keep going."

They floated around another bend in the river and saw the remains of a Spanish-style ranch house, now a tumbled assembly of pitiful burnt ruins sprawling near the water.

Wild Indians charged around the area looking for loot and survivors. Pin-cushioned bodies were scattered among the charred wreckage as a column of smoke reached skyward. It was a terrifying scene of carnage and ferocity.

Everyone nervously held their breath as the upcoming scene of rampaging warriors, the sounds of their war cries and scattered shots grew closer.

"We should get off the river." whispered Tom, licking his lips, but before Sam could answer, green and black painted faces turned towards them, and a few natives drifted toward the riverbank, weapons at the ready.

"Wouldn't help, they'd find us anyway. Maybe we can get by them. Relax. Don't make eye contact."

The raft edged closer. Indians gathered on the bank, waiting ominously, spears, bows and blowguns in hand. The raft crew was tense and helpless as they came abreast of the marauders—yards apart—face to face. Suddenly, Linda smiled and waved. Maria quickly took up the pretense, calling out in a native tongue, joking with the war party. The braves smiled and waved back, then turned away to continue their plundering as the raft swept by.

Tom was incredulous. "My God, Linda, are you crazy? You almost got us all killed."

"No, she didn't," smiled Sam. "She saved our lives. You're pretty handy to have around, pal, even if you are crazy."

Linda smiled back at Sam, shaking her head from side to side and grinning like a little kid saying, "I told you so."

• • • ● • ● ● • • •

More days passed, and the rains increased. First, large billowing dark clouds would materialize to blanket the jungle, always accompanied by the steady advance of lightning and peels of thunder. Then the light patter of a thin drizzle, with rain tapping the broad leaves and river water, and in a few moments building to a roaring downpour.

Their routine changed with the weather. At the first signs of a storm, Sam would search for a spot that might offer the best protection and head for shore. There, they would scramble to find themselves hide-a-ways among the trees—but escape from the water was impossible. Water ran down the branches and trunks to form rivulets that surged around roots, and their feet.

The storms brought other dangers as well. Snakes, driven from the brush, swam through the fresh streams seeking their own shelter, sometimes coming perilously close.

After the storms had passed, there was a secondary rainfall, as the sheltering trees shed the water accumulated on their leaves. The change in temperature and humidity had its effects also, causing a ground fog to rise, shrouding the jungle in a dewy mist, rendering the landscape surreal and mysterious.

Maria was best accustomed to her native weather, but Linda took it the worst. Sticking to her disguise, she became increasingly ill because of her exposure and being constantly soaked.

One afternoon, as they sought shelter during a downpour, Sam sat in a tangle of roots, head down, thinking. He admired Linda more and more. She had shown real courage at the slaver camp by hitting Soto, and later, when she had hailed the wild Indians at the burning plantation. Now, sick or not, she was still game, uncomplaining, a real trooper. He couldn't help himself. He liked her more than he dared to admit, even though she was keeping her distance.

Without reason, he looked up and saw her. She was leaning against a wet tree trunk, her arms folded across her chest for warmth, her hair quivering, signaling her cold. She glanced at him and smiled, a sad-eyed smile with chattering teeth.

The urge to hold her was irresistible. He rose, and they stood together, their eyes meeting. He slowly folded her into his arms, felt her shudder as his warmth encircled her body. Her arms pulled him closer. Her head pressed into his shoulder, and he could feel her breath on his neck. They pulled together as tightly as they could, sharing their body heat, trembling against each other, squeezing, shivering, melting together. Their lips brushed, found each other's—it made them warmer. Yearning kindled, they began to glue together with long, slow kisses, groggy, time suspending...blissful.

At last, the rain ebbed, the roar of falling water subsided. Embarrassed, they let each other go apologetically. This wasn't supposed to happen. It was just one of those things. They would forget about it. Lock the memory of those kisses away in their hearts. Go on without each other.

• • • ● • ● • • •

Maria was the first to give voice to what was obvious to them all. "Sam," she whispered, pointing to Linda who sat slumped over amidships, "Linda very sick."

Sam could see that. They had covered her with the few pieces of clothing they had. Still, she had become more and more listless. She would spend the day holding the scraps of clothing around her shoulders while she shivered; and nights had been spent trying to keep her warm, even as fires were difficult in the jungle wetness.

Sam nodded. He knew it would still be several days to the mission and he could see Linda getting worse. He had felt they couldn't waste any time stopping, without medicine of any kind to treat her—so he had opted to get to the mission as fast as he could. Now it looked as though they were running out of time to save her.

It was heartbreaking, but Sam didn't have another answer until he heard Maria say, "Maybe we could go to my village. It close. We have powerful medicine man. Help her get better."

Sam knew it would take them out of the way, for who knew how long? But that seemed to be the best answer.

He let Maria guide him. She indicated a small tributary screened by trees, and he steered their raft through shrubbery that protected its entrance. He knew he would have missed it if he had been by himself.

The tributary became more of a swamp, studded with trees that shut out all but narrow shafts of sunlight. Sam poled through the semi-darkness, surrounded by animal cries and bird calls, mindful of the large crocodiles that drifted lazily in the surrounding shallows, and the low-hanging branches that might shelter snakes or spiders. The swamp gradually thinned away, and the river became itself again.

"Soon now," Maria said excitedly.

They saw a cluster of stilted huts rising out of the swamp's edge. They had reached Maria's village.

• • • • • • • • • •

Sam docked the raft, and the natives assembled spontaneously hailing Maria, happily surprised by her arrival.

Sam could tell by Maria's actions that she was telling her people the story of her capture and their escape. As she spoke, the villagers looked back and forth between Maria and Sam and the others with increasing smiles.

Once Maria had finished recounting the story of her adventure, grateful villagers led the three to a large thatch hut, raised six feet by sturdy bamboo columns. They climbed the ladder and entered, almost immediately feeling the warmth of the central fire in the smoky interior.

Maria returned with a long piece of trade cloth which she gave to Linda to wrap around herself, sarong-like. And for the first time in days, Linda slept soundly, relatively dry, and definitely warmer, in spite of the afternoon rain.

Sam sat by the door looking out into the storm battered village, wishing the sounds of pounding rain and splashing water could erase the memory of their kiss. But the beating torrent seemed to drive it deeper into his thoughts until it was hard to think of anything else. He could feel his desire for her grow with a deep yearning that was stomach wrenching, but to what end?

It's pointless, he thought, *hopeless.* Still, he couldn't look at her laying there, helpless, ill, suffering, without wanting to crush her in his arms and smother her with kisses. *I'm crazy,* he thought, *Love*sick, *dopey, crazy. It's no use, no good,* he kept telling himself. *I have to get her out of my system—I have to, before I make a fool of myself.*

For her part, when Linda would wake, she would stare into the fire, smell the smoke, and remember the warmth of their embrace. She knew she had to stop thinking about him. She had to. To let herself fall in love would ruin everything. Meeting him was just a mistake. It was all just a stupid mistake, a maddening unwanted distraction.

Tom sat alone, still watching both of them. They were acting strange. They avoided each other, both unusually quiet. What had happened he wondered? Whatever it was, it seemed to have driven them apart. That was good. Now all he had to do was regain her confidence.

But, when he tried to speak to her, she seemed listless, uninterested. It must be a sickness of some sort, he thought. She must have come down with something out there in the jungle, in the rain. Whatever it was, he would wait it out.

None of them never really noticed the old man who spent much of his time sitting in the corner, watching them all. He was painted black from the mouth down, wore a crown of toucan bills, and when he moved, his necklace of armadillo claws would rattle on his bony chest. He always seemed to be softly chanting and beating on his small reptile hide drum.

· · · ●· ● · · ·

One night, after they had all fallen asleep, Maria woke Linda and Sam and told them to follow her, that the medicine man had prepared a tonic for them. When they asked about Tom, Maria shook her head, "Medicine man say, he not have same sickness. Other medicine for him."

They followed Maria along a narrow slippery path, between thatch huts whose roofs still dripped rainwater, until they reached a small, stilted one. They climbed the bamboo stairs a few feet and entered. Inside there was a small fire burning, and the same old man with the toucan head-dress they recognized from the other hut, where he had sat, drummed, and looked after them.

They were bidden to seat themselves by the fire and an assistant brought two wooden bowls containing a strong-smelling liquid.

"What do you think it is, Sam?" she asked.

"I don't know," he answered, raising his bowl to his nose. "It's not chicha, that's for sure."

"Swallow and smile?"

"I guess," he shrugged. "He looks friendly enough."

They regarded the medicine man, who smiled at them and kept chanting, keeping a droning, barely audible rhythm on his drum.

They drank the sticky, foul-smelling medicine, then reclined on sleeping mats on either side of the fire.

Almost immediately, Linda was overtaken by a strong nauseating sensation. She wanted to retch but couldn't move except to draw her knees up towards her middle. At last, her stomach convulsed, and she gagged, but still felt paralyzed. A calming dizziness overcame her, and her surroundings began to shimmer and come alive.

First, green vines wound up through the floor to entrap her, holding her, their tendrils turning into green children, who spoke in a foreign, sing-song language she seemed to understand, as they danced around her, telling her to relax, to accept a message that a powerful spirit was showing her. She felt pervaded by a web of glowing plasma that stretched to infinity, connecting her with a powerful life-source that was transferring its energy into her, helping her, healing her.

Then she saw Sam was also connected. Connected together, they were bound for eternity in a poetic, undulating, cosmic field of beatitude.

Then there was a growl, and a large black leopard, head down, yellow eyes glowing, circled the fire to lay at her side. It scratched itself against her, rolling on its back and pawed the emptiness. She petted it, ran her fingers lovingly back and forth against its silky black fur, looked into its glowing yellow eyes as it growl-purred and licked the air. She lapsed into unconsciousness.

Waking at dawn, Linda experienced a bitter after taste, crawled to the doorway, and expelled a stomach full of dark bile. Drained, it took her time to catch her breath, and when she did, she crawled weakly back to her place by the fire. There she saw a disturbed mat and large muddy cat tracks next to where she had been laying. She swooned.

· · · ●·●·● ·· ·

Sometime later, the sound of the downpour woke them both. They looked at each other across the small fire with blank stares.

What was his dream like? she wondered. *Could it have been like mine?*

Sam said nothing, only lowered his head.

They returned to their places in the main hut, where they lounged in troubled silence for a few more days, until eventually, Sam nudged her with his foot. "You okay to travel?" he asked.

"Hu-huh, I think so," she returned listlessly.

"We better get going then."

Maria arranged for them to have a canoe in place of the balsa raft that had brought them. It was filled with food and supplies, hammocks, and weapons to hunt with.

The villagers stood at the water's edge to wish them a safe journey.

Maria stayed behind, having found a beau to marry. She smiled and waved most of all.

• • • ● •● ● ● •• •

The next few days on the river passed slowly, as the adrenalin rush, inspired by their flight from danger, was now gone.

Their words were few, and Tom noticed that Sam and Linda seemed less animated, less drawn to each other, both spending much of their time in solitary contemplation. When Tom tried to draw Linda out of her far-away looks and into conversation, he continued to be met with a dim smile and a profound disinterest.

Neglected, Tom quietly seethed with a growing anger, mostly aimed at Sam—all this was Sam's fault. Sam had come between him and Linda, even now that they weren't speaking, it had something to do with Sam. Sam had to go. He would get his revenge. After all, he was the superior person and the one rightfully entitled to Linda's affection. It was just a matter of time.

Chapter 15

The darkness of Father Julian's room was broken by a shaft of light, as the priest's door was opened by Bernardo, a mission boy.

"Padre?"

Father Julian woke with a start, rubbed his eyes, and reached for his Spanish breastplate. He heard the sound of peeling church bells.

"*Enamigos? Indios malos?*"

"No, Padre. *Extranjeros, con* Sam."

"Sam? *Seguro?*" Father Julian smiled and crossed himself as he hurriedly dressed.

Father Julian followed the line of torches and arrived at the dock in time to see native acolytes surrounding a happy, but tired crew. Sam and Father Julian embraced in the warm firelight, and they all introduced themselves.

"Thank God, it's good to see you all made it safely. You must be starving," said Father Julian

"I'd like a nap first, and some hot water, and maybe a razor," Sam said, rubbing his beard.

"Likewise, please," came Tom.

"I hate to ask, but could I get a bath, and maybe some dry clothes?" asked Linda.

"Of course, of course. We can do all of that, especially if you don't mind bathing in an old wine vat. We use it for baptisms, but I'll get it filled with hot water for you. Come, I'll have you shown to rooms and get the water started."

They were led to separate adjoining rooms along the long low wing of cells. The doors sat behind adobe arches and under a Spanish tile roof, now partially covered with flowering vines.

"Please," coaxed Father Julian, "Relax, rest. Should you want anything, just call for Bernardo. I'll get the kitchen started. Food will be ready when you are."

Linda was taken to an outside room at the end of the long wing, where a large wine vat had been cut in half. A trellis of fragrant orchids served as a screen for the wine vat bathtub. Once filled with hot water by neophytes, she undressed in the darkness and immersed herself in the bath. Almost immediately, she relaxed, feeling the aches and pains of her journey gradually subside, the hot steam adoring her face and clearing her mind.

Sam, she thought, *What about Sam? What am I going to do?*

She had started into the Amazon with the clear-headed purpose of finding Truman or treasure, definitely not romance. "No distractions", she had vowed. Now she found herself agonizingly torn. The memory of the kiss they had shared in the jungle still conjured a powerful, smoldering desire. She had struggled to ignore it, but try as she might, she couldn't forget those passion-filled moments in the rain and the feeling of being complete in his arms.

And that dream she had. How strange it was. It seemed to tell her...tell her what? That they were meant for each other? How corny, how stupid...and yet...would she trade a fortune for his love? Did he love her in the same way, or had he just been excited by her near nudity, and wanted to possess her sexually? It had happened before—she had given her heart a few times and been walked out on. She knew the hurt and hated the memory.

Maybe that's why I never really committed myself to Truman, not really. Oh, I don't want to think about all that anymore, she said to herself, sinking into the hot water. She felt tired of going crazy. She had spent the days since leaving Maria's village withdrawn in silent contemplation, afraid to look at him.

Now she decided, "Hell, if it's really that important to me, I have to find out the truth—somehow, I have to find out."

• • • •• • • •• •

Hours passed. Sam woke to the sound of crickets and frogs, and soon there was a knock at his door, and Bernardo's soft voice, "Dinner, *señor*?"

"Okay, thanks." Sam mumbled as he sat up and stretched.

He crossed to the small table where he splashed cold water on his face from an enameled basin and regarded himself in a small, dirty mirror as he toweled himself dry. He looked different, better. Washed and shaved, he started running a wooden comb through his hair, studying his reflection, watching himself as he would another person.

How's this going to end? he wondered. *Maybe I should stay here and let Linda and Tom go on with a couple of mission Indians—or maybe I should go on, let them enjoy the comforts of life with Father Julian and wait for the mail boat to take them downriver in safety. Either way, I can't spend any more time around Linda.*

Finished, he dropped the comb.

If I spend more time around her, I'll do something stupid, say something stupid, just make a fool of myself. Crap! He let his fist strike the table. *I knew she was going to be trouble—I knew it the minute I saw her.*

He closed his eyes and remembered the first instant he saw her face, all dirty and breathless and beautiful.

"Crap," he said again, dropping his head and striking the table a second time.

· · · ● ● · ● ● · ·

After a while, Sam, wearing clean, loose, white mission clothing, entered the dining room to find Tom and Father Julian sitting at the long dining table in the amber glow of a line of hissing gasoline pressure lamps.

"Ah, Sam." Father Julian greeted him, standing.

"Padre, Tom..."

The monk waved him to the table and poured him a small glass of wine.

"I must say, Sam, you look better than the last time I saw you."

"Thanks, Padre. I sure feel better," he said, running a hand across his smooth face as he took his seat.

"You must share your secret with me—" Father Julian froze in mid-sentence.

Sam and Tom followed his gaze to the doorway, where Linda stood, smiling somewhat bashfully, wearing an old Gibson Girl wedding dress, all white lace and gauze and tiny pink ribbon trim. Her blond hair, humidity curled, haloing around her face, still blushing rosily from her hot bath, she looked breathtakingly natural—yet uncertain, and all the men stood in various postures of surprise as she crossed to the table.

"A vision of loveliness, *señorita*..." said the monk, holding his hand over his heart and bowing.

"Yes, Linda, quite alluring," Tom's voice was somewhat cool. Sam stood speechless, entranced...finally blinking away.

She reached the table, smiling, her hands spreading the dress fabric. "It's beautiful, Padre," she said softly. "I hope you don't mind me wearing it."

Bernardo pulled a chair, and she sat next to Tom, across from Sam and Father Julian.

"Not at all, not at all. The poor old thing. We save it for the weddings. It doesn't get much use, I'm afraid. Your beauty does it great honor." He bowed again, sitting.

"Thank you, Padre. I didn't know priests, or monks, could be so flattering."

Bernardo started serving around the table, ladling stew into wooden bowls.

"Well, after all, I am Spanish," the monk smiled.

Sam and Linda looked at each other, unsuccessfully trying to hide their affection.

Tom spoke quickly to break the spell. "The Father and I were talking earlier, and guess what? Great news! There's a supply boat running," he said, obviously happy.

"In fact, it left a few days ago, but—" began Father Julian.

"But it ran aground, just downriver. They're working on it now and we should be able to leave in a day or two," said Tom, a little too fast, unable to cloak his relief. He patted her hand, retrieving her attention.

"How long is the trip to Iquitos?" asked Linda quietly.

"A few days," said Sam.

"With any luck, we can be on our way out of this god-forsaken place and back to New York in less than a week," said Tom, trying to ignore the obvious emotional looks flashing between Sam and Linda.

"That is good news," she said, not really meaning it.

The energy at the table collapsed. Father Julian tried to rescue a happy mood. Taking a spoonful, he smiled, "I hope the food meets with your approval...down here it passes for chicken."

"Thank you, Padre. Whatever it is, it tastes as good as anything I've ever eaten, in Topeka, New York, or Paris, for that matter," said Linda.

The priest beamed. "I've never been to New York; but Paris ...ahh, what a city. You know it too, eh, Sam?"

"I've been there," he said without looking up.

"Really?" asked Linda, surprised and excited to find they had something in common. "Isn't it wonderful? Where did you stay?"

"Trenches mostly," he said quietly, without looking up.

"Oh, the war...." She realized at once that Sam must have been one of America's beautiful young boys. Boys that had marched off singing "Over There", to fight the war to end all wars, only to suffer unspeakable horrors, then return, damaged and broken, to an ungrateful nation—filling the ranks of forgotten men. Maybe that explained his self-exile to the jungle. The insight saddened her.

Sam realized his voice had revealed a streak of self-pity, usually buried beneath a façade of irreverence, and sought to dispel the oppressiveness with humor.

"Interminable spans of boredom punctuated by short periods of intense violence." He tried to say it lightly, but it only served to expose more hurt. "I got to town a few times. Saw some pretty interesting places. I don't think you'd know any of them."

"I wouldn't be so sure—" she smiled.

Tom rushed to cut her off. "Ahh, Padre. That was good."

"Thank you," accepted the monk, happy for the restoration of normalcy. "I can't offer you much for dessert. A little fruit and brandy perhaps...well, it tastes like brandy."

Linda looked away. "Father, does that guitar work?" she asked brightly, pointing to the instrument that hung on the wall.

"I think so, though it's quite out of tune, I'm afraid."

"Mind if I try?" she asked.

"Not at all, not at all. I'll get it for you."

Father Julian stood, so did Linda.

"I'll get it, Father. You pour the brandy," she said, licking her fingers as she retrieved the guitar from the wall, then returned to put her foot on a chair and swing the instrument up onto her knee.

She smiled at Sam as she tuned up, giving Father Julian time to pour and hand out glasses of amber liquid. "It's been a long time...well, here goes."

She strummed a couple of opening chords as she cleared her throat, then, to everyone's surprise, she opened into a French cabaret song. Her voice was as throaty and rich and vibrant as it was unexpected, and the guttural French words of love rolled off her tongue directly at Sam.

Sam was mesmerized, captivated, his face completely open with adoration, only slightly less so the Padre, who remembered Sam's long-ago remark of needing a musical angel—and here she was. Sam had brought her without knowing it—by what amazing power, he wondered.

Tom sat stiffly, using every ounce of strength he possessed not to stomp out in a fit of jealous rage at the sight of Linda throwing herself at Sam with her slutty singing or the sight of Sam's glistening eyes.

• • • • • • • • • •

Later, the evening over, Sam, Linda, and a protective Tom walked along in silence, under the vine covered colonnade, to their rooms.

"Well, this is where I get off," announced Sam, reaching his door.

"The moon's up," she said.

"So it is," intruded Tom, "A good night for a walk, hey, Linda?"

But Sam and Linda only had eyes for each other. He picked a flower and placed it behind her ear. "You're an amazing piece of work, even if you are a crazy broad."

She took the flower from her ear, smelled it, put it back, "So are you, you big lunk."

"Yes, well, I think we're all pretty amazing, considering what we just came through, don't you?" Tom touched Linda's arm, hating to have to just stand there, watching them moon over each other, sick to reclaim Linda's attention, and his position of importance and influence in her life.

Sam looked at her a moment. "Look." He said, "I know this is none of my business but...but don't slow down, don't look back. Get on that mail boat and get out of here while you have the chance."

"It's not that easy." She let her eyes drop. "I can't go back empty-handed. I want to find out if I'm married or free, rich or poor...and maybe something else too," she said, looking at him.

"Being alive is more important than any of that." Then he said quietly, "goodnight."

He turned slowly and went into his room, softly closing the door behind him.

Linda and Tom were left standing together alone.

Tom began immediately, "Yes, you are quite amazing, Linda. I never knew you spoke French, or played the guitar, for that matter." His insides quaked. They had just played their little love scene in front of him, ignoring him as if he didn't exist, diminishing him, humiliating him to his face. He began to hate

Linda, almost as much as he hated Sam; but he couldn't let his emotions get in the way of a bigger game. If he couldn't have her affection, he could still have her money.

"Say, tell you what." He intoned, "Maybe I can liberate a bottle of wine from the kitchen and we—"

"I'm sorry Tom," she waved him off, distracted, "not tonight. I have something to think about. I'll see you tomorrow."

She finished abruptly and left him standing alone in the moonlight, his stomach churning with bitterness and defeat.

· · · ● · ● · ● · · ·

Sam lay awake on his bunk, shirtless. The small room was hot and stuffy, but that wasn't the cause of his sleeplessness.

He heard a soft scratching on his door. He knew it was her. He wanted to open the door—knew he shouldn't. The scratching became more determined, more persistent.

He swung his legs to the floor and took a few steps. He ran his fingers through his hair. *If I let her in,* he thought, *I'll get hurt again, really hurt.* He knew the suffering would be terrible if things went wrong, and they were sure to. *The hell with it!* He stepped to the door...opened it.

There she stood, in the moonlight, in that white dress, looking angelic.

"What?" he asked softly.

She slipped inside, turned quickly, bolted the door, then turned back.

"You know what, you big lunk." came breathless words. Eyes half closed, she bit her lower lip. His hands found her sides, he felt her ribs, felt her suck breath in and out. He drew her closer, inhaling her fragrance, closing his eyes, pressing his lips to her forehead.

"You better get out of here. Right now!" he whispered hoarsely.

"Why?" she asked, her fingernails raking his bare stomach. He shuttered, "cause if you stay any longer, I'm going to kiss your face off," he choked.

"You're wasting time," her voice, almost groggy.

They crushed together eagerly, with an intense wet twisting kiss, fueled by mutual passion born of pent-up desire.

"Help me out of this thing," she moaned. "I don't want to ruin the padre's dress."

They fell onto the bunk in each other's arms, devouring each other hungrily, heedless of anything and everything but themselves. At times they would lay together, kissing gently, saying all the love words, and making all the pledges they knew—then rekindling their appetites, exhausting themselves again, insatiably. All under the sightless gaze of the plaster Madonna with her outstretched arms.

Tom sat on his bunk in the next room, overhearing almost everything, even through the thick adobe walls. Hot tears streamed down his cheeks. He held his head in his hands, sometimes beating his fists against his temples, trying to banish the sordid images the sounds provoked.

Gradually, tormented by his inner agony, he determined to destroy Sam, kill him if possible, and maybe kill Linda too.

Chapter 16

The next morning, Linda woke to the sounds of birds screeching and monkey chatter. Daylight streamed in through the cracks around the window coverings, giving the room a soft glow. She realized it must be quite late. Feeling dreamy and peaceful, her first thoughts went to Sam. He did love her, and she loved him.

The hell with everything else, she thought, feeling a delicious buoyancy as she dropped the one-piece native sack dress over her head. *God, I'm hungry,* came her second thought as she combed her hair.

Linda ambled into the Mission dining room to find Father Julian hovering over the wood-burning oven next to Bernardo.

"Good morning," she called out, smiling.

Julian turned and saw her, appraised her a moment. "Do you feel alright?" He asked, a little concern in his voice.

"I feel fine," she replied. "Why?"

"You look a bit flushed. In fact, I would say glowing."

Suddenly embarrassed, she fanned herself with her hand. "Woosh," she said, "I guess my motor's running a little hot this morning."

An unintended good-natured laugh broke from the frier's lips, "Well, we can eat any time," he said, turning back to his cooking, "The boys won't be joining us."

"Oh, why not?" she asked, sitting at the table.

"Sam came in this morning looking happier than I've ever seen him, said he wasn't very hungry and went to help the men fix the boat...Tom went too."

"I guess I'm not very hungry either. Funny, I thought I was."

"Well, I assume you're excited about leaving."

Linda sat at the table and said nothing.

"You're so quiet, my dear. What's wrong? You should be happy to be leaving this place."

"I know, but so much has changed. Nothing is the way I thought it would be. I guess I'm just confused, happily confused," she said, smiling.

"Yes, life has a way of reproving us sometimes. You know what they say, 'If you want to make God laugh, tell him your plans'."

They both chuckled, but the monk saw something serious in her eyes. "Would you like to tell me what's troubling you?" he asked, taking a close chair.

"It's a long story," she answered, looking down, thinking about everything that had happened.

"Well, time we have in abundance. Please, start at the beginning."

Linda cradled her chin in her hands.... "Well, I guess it all started in New York—gee, it seems like a million years ago..."

• • • ●• ● ● • •

The forty-foot mail boat rested partially out of water. It was stuck on a sandbar that had appeared when the river, swollen by the rains, had drained to its normal level. The two-man crew, and four soldier guards worked to repair her bottom. The captain, an old river dog with a tobacco-stained beard, sat in the shade of a makeshift lean-to.

Sam, smiling, shirtless, ax in hand, assembled a work party of mission Indians.

Tom stood relaxed, watching, hands in his pockets. "You sure I can't help?" he asked with false enthusiasm.

"Don't worry about it," smiled Sam, "we'll have this done in no time."

"I didn't realize you were so anxious to leave," said Tom, feeling another twist of jealousy, noticing the parallel red welts on Sam's back that evidenced Linda's passionate raking fingernails.

"You kidding? The sooner I get Linda out of here, the sooner I can help her clear up her life.... My life.... Our life."

Tom couldn't mistake the inference. "What? What do you mean, our lives?" he said, suddenly attentive.

Sam, grinning like a schoolboy, shouted, "Use a little imagination, pal." Then to the waiting helpers, "come-on boys, let's go!" He led the work-party away into the jungle.

Tom watched them leave, nervousness rising. He hated the idea of Linda giving herself to Sam. He had considered it to have been an escapade, a sexual indiscretion born of loneliness; regrettable, but not necessarily fatal to his relationship with her.

Sam's comment seemed to indicate something more serious. Was this in her mind also? He knew he had to quickly create a plan which could both separate them from each other and allow him to get her safely away, out of the Amazon completely. He had to use Sam's weakness, and of course, Linda was Sam's weakness. It wasn't long before Tom, smiling, crossed to the captain. "Can I use the radio to call Iquitos?"

"Of course, *señor*." The captain said lazily, pointing to the ship with his palm fan, "Help yourself."

Tom climbed the gangway and crossed the creaky wooden deck to the cabin, where he sat at the portable shortwave set, put on the headphones, and spoke into the microphone.

"Hello...patch this into World Rubber, can you?"

"Right away," came the hollow response.

• • • • • • • • • •

Father Julian sat quietly as Linda finished her story.

"So, what do I do now? Keep looking, or forget the whole thing and start a new life with Sam?" She fell silent, her eyes asking for a response that would make sense of her struggle.

Father Julian said nothing for a moment...then, "This, I cannot answer...but the Indians would say that the curi-puri is very strong in your story."

"What's that supposed to mean?"

"Where should I start? Curi-puri? Fate, destiny, coincidence? We might argue the nature of it, but a supernatural process to be sure—something like divine retribution, or 'karma' as the heathens call it. You see, much of your story perplexes me. For instance, we call this mission La Merced, but in the days of the conquistadors, this place was called Cabo de Christos."

Linda sat up excitedly. "Then I've found it. Father, have you heard of my husband, Truman?

"Yes, and that's another thing that bothers me, although I should be happy to give you news of him. He was here. It was several months ago. He was sick with the fever and, more I think, tormented by something, his very soul was in deep agony. He spoke from his delirium of being unworthy to receive God's treasure—that he had been responsible for violating the spirit of the land. That in his greed for wealth, he was destroying the Garden of Eden. It was all so confusing." Father Julian sighed, shrugged, "Then, one day, he was gone."

"But where, how?" she asked, grabbing his hand.

The monk shook his head, "He left before he was well, crept away into the night. It was about that time that the slaves begin to revolt."

"Then he's alive...." She sat back, her eyes searching empty space.

"Perhaps. That was some time ago," the monk crossed himself. "But yes, by the grace of God. Later, others came looking for him, very evil-looking men."

Linda threw the monk a questioning look.

"It seems everyone turned against him. Plantation owners, Indians...." He looked away, shook his head at the memory. "And, another thing, your meeting Sam was nothing short of a miracle."

"Yes, I know," she said, her heart agreeing.

The monk settled in thought a moment, then, was quickly aroused. "I almost forgot. Your husband left a small knapsack, not much really. I'll have it taken to your quarters."

Linda hurried back to her room and soon heard a soft knock at the door. She opened it to find Bernardo, who, smiling, handed her a heavily used khaki canvas rucksack. She thanked him as she closed the door, then placed the bag on the small table under the window.

She stood there, staring at Truman's rucksack, keyed with hope, afraid of finding nothing. Finally, praying for something, anything helpful, she opened the bag. Her nervous fingers unbuckled the pockets, and she dumped the meager contents out, littering the table in front of her. She sat and slowly picked through the items. There were a few personal things, a shirt, some socks, nothing of interest or value.

She sat back, defeated, and with a deep sigh of disappointment, began stuffing Truman's things back into the bag—when she felt something hard. Quickly, she examined the interior and found a hidden pocket. Excitement rising, she searched it, and with trembling hands, withdrew a soiled, water-proofed banker's envelope. She gently opened it, and carefully withdrew the contents, an ancient and discolored paper map, folded and creased from use, fragile but still readable.

This must be the map that was torn from Truman's book, she guessed. Her finger traced the line of the river, and she found her position.

Linda was suddenly startled by a loud knock at the door. She quickly folded the map and stuck it in her pocket. "Yes?" she said.

"It's me," came Tom's voice. "May I come in?"

"Sure."

Tom looked in high-spirits, happier than she had seen him in days.

"Well, looks like everything is set for tomorrow," he said, "and I've called the company and booked two tickets for New York—"

"I'm not turning back," she said.

"What? But surely you can't mean that, not after everything we've just been through."

"Tom, Brother Julian said that Truman was here. He was sick with fever."

"All the more reason to go home. Don't you see? He must have died out there somewhere," he gestured with his hand, growing aggravated, "You'll never find any evidence now."

"It's not that. All this time I hated Truman because I thought he ran out on me, but he was sick and couldn't help himself. If he's alive, then I'm still his wife, whether I love him or not, I have to try and find him, see if I can help him."

Tom's anger rose. Once again, he stood to be thwarted by circumstance. "What can you do? The company has had skilled men out looking for weeks...and nothing."

"Yes, but I know where he went."

"Linda, please, don't start that again. Don't you understand? This has gone on long enough."

"Alright then. I have another reason to keep going...I have to find out if I'm married or not, because I want to marry Sam. There, I've said it."

Tom's face dropped. "But, but that's madness!"

"Maybe it is, I don't care. I know it sounds crazy. It's been driving me nuts, too...but now I'm sure and I don't care if I'm rich or poor as long as I'm with him."

Tom paused, retreated behind a questioning voice. "Does he know how you feel?" He asked, introducing doubt to buy time, realizing his chances were slipping from his grasp.

"Well, I haven't proposed, if that's what you mean."

"Then do me one favor. Wait until we get back to Iquitos. See if he feels the same way about you before you lose your head. I don't want to see you make a mistake that could ruin your life," he purred smoothly, elements of a plan drawing together in his mind.

"Okay, Tom, but it won't matter."

"Maybe not. But if, when we get to Iquitos, you still want to stay on...well then, I promise to try to help you. Fair enough?"

He could see her jaw flexing as she nodded and stuck out her hand. "Okay, Tom, deal."

Tom took his time walking back. "This is it," he thought, "If I'm to do anything, it has to be now."

The plan suggesting itself to him was deliciously simple and manipulative, sure to poison their relationship and set them against each other.

Tom allowed himself a laugh, inwardly cheered at his own cleverness.

· · · ● · ● · ● · · ·

He returned to the boat in time to see Sam and the men launch it. The captain stood in his cabin holding the whistle chain, waiting to give the signal to the mate, who stood astern by the engine. Sam and the work-gang had lain a large trunk on the bar next to the hull, then they used smaller poles, set over the trunk and under the hull, to leverage the boat off the bar. When all was ready, Sam yelled at the skipper, who blew the whistle, signaling the mate to throw power to the propeller, which quickly churned the water at the ship's stern as the men plied their poles. Between everyone's efforts, the boat slid backwards and floated off the bar, bobbing freely as the whistle tooted and the men cheered victoriously.

Tom hailed Sam. "Can you give me a minute?" he said, using his most concerned tone.

They walked together towards the mission. Tom began, "What you're doing to Linda is wrong and you know it!" he said plaintively.

"You better mind your own business, pal," said Sam.

"I mean it. Think about what's happening. Think about her..." Tom put his hand on Sam's arm, stopping him. "Look, you're a decent sort of fellow. I can understand the attractiveness—down here—but what if she falls in love with you? What will you do? Take her to Paris, New York, or get a little place around here somewhere?" He waved his hand, indicating the jungle for emphasis. "The jungle will kill her, you said so yourself." Tom backed off a bit, watching Sam's reaction.

Sam got the message. He had been struggling all morning with that very question. He knew she was too good for him; he knew that it might all end in heartache. He had just wished for a little more time of happiness, and a softer fall.

Sam started away, but Tom felt he had to push it a bit more. "She doesn't belong down here," he continued, following Sam, trying to be as sincere and concerned as he could, almost pleading, "She's a thoroughbred. She belongs with her kind, not living down here in squalor like a hunted animal. Don't make it any harder for her to leave." They stopped again. "I know it's asking a lot, but try to put her happiness ahead of yours...." he trailed off, watching Sam.

Sam waved Tom away. "Okay, okay. You made your point. I'll do what I can...but you better take her out of here fast and you better take her far away."

"There'll be a plane waiting at Iquitos to fly her home to New York. Thanks, Sam, you're doing the right thing."

"Yeah, yeah," Sam mumbled, knowing that when anyone said, "you're doing the right thing", they always meant the right thing for someone else.

Tom watched Sam walk away, head down, shoulders slumping. *The poor fool*, he thought. He was glad that he had taken acting classes in preparation for jury presentation. He had calculated Sam's reaction correctly. Hit him right in his most venerable spot, his emotional solar plexus.

"God, I'm good," he flattered himself. Now to get back in control of Linda, and back on his home ground in New York, and business negotiation. He'd come out alright, after all, he was still the superior person in all this.

Sam disappeared the rest of the day. He first went to his room, where he lay on his bunk. He could still smell Linda on his blanket. He scrunched it up to his face. After a while, he gathered his things and headed for the boat.

• • • ● • ● • • •

Linda looked for Sam at dinner but couldn't find him. Tom hid innocently behind his Cheshire cat smile, feigning innocence as to what might have happened.

Later, Linda lay in her bunk, sleepless and restless with worry about Sam's disappearance. She was bursting with the news of Truman and the discovery of his map. She felt sure he would support her. That they would go on together, finding whatever, and more importantly, start a new future.

Chapter 17

They boarded the mail-boat early. It surprised Linda to see Sam, already aboard, sitting with the soldiers at the bow. She was more surprised to see him drunk.

Friar Julian and the rest of the mission Indians waved good-bye as the mail boat, whistle blowing, chugged its way out into the main stream, and headed down-river.

Sam sat with the four soldiers in the bow where they practiced target shooting with a drum-fed Lewis gun. They passed a bottle and cheered each other on, as the machine-gun chattered loudly, and bullets splashed around distant floating logs. Linda and Tom sat astern under a canvas canopy, Sam ignoring them both.

After a while, Tom appeared to have dozed off. But Linda continued to study Sam with concern. *What was wrong?* she wondered. Finally, compelled by equal parts of curiosity and excitement, she walked to the bow and tried to get Sam's attention between drinks and shots.

"Sam?" she said.

"Yeah?"

"I'd like to talk to you."

"Go ahead on."

"Not here...it's a secret."

"Awww, honey, these old boys don't care. Say any damn thing you want."

She didn't like it, but she could see it wasn't going to get any better. "Sam, I found out something at the mission. Father Julian told me that it used to be Cabo de Christos...."

Sam gave her a quizzed look.

She went on quickly, "Don't you see? Truman's map to El Dorado started at Cabo de Christos. The map from his book—"

"Awww," he started, turning back to shoot, "a map's nothing but a lot of names written on paper...there ain't nothing out there but hard times and death."

"There is, Sam, up there in the mountains...."

Sam held a beat, then broke into drunken laughter. The soldiers joined him. Linda could feel her face flush with embarrassment. She bit her thumb nail.

Sam pulled himself to his feet, swaying badly, he called out to the ship's captain. "Yo, skipper, ever heard of El Dorado?"

Linda was horrified. "Sam!"

The captain nodded, "Si, *señor*, of course, everyone has."

"Tell this little city girl about it, will ya?"

The captain took on the air of an impresario, chin up, arms and hands gesturing, "A fabulous treasure, *señora*...from the Inca times. A lost city guarded by Amazon women. Up there, in the mountains. That's why they call this jungle the Amazon."

He finished with a smile, bowing slightly as though he expected applause.

Sam looked at her condescendingly. Asked the captain, "Ever seen a map?"

"Oh *si*, *señor*," the captain went on, seriously, "They sell many in the marketplace, but in Iquitos I know a very old man who has one. A real one! From the time of the conquistadors."

"How much?" asked Sam, his eyes boring into hers.

"Oh, I don't know, *señor*... Maybe twenty *oros*."

Sam scowled at Linda, rubbing it in. "Twenty *oros*. Five bucks. That's what all your secret information bullshit is worth."

Suffering the sting of betrayal and humiliation, unwanted tears began to flow down her cheeks, but she stood her ground. "Why are you doing this, Sam? I thought we made a pretty good team—"

Still a little unsteady, he stood facing her, eyes red, "When are you gonna wise up? Go home. There's nothing for you down here...nothing. Just because you were easy pickings in the jungle—"

Her face reddened. She gasped and slapped him. Bit her lip. Eyebrows knitted, she slapped him again. Tried a third time, and he grabbed her wrists, stopping her, staring her down.

Her eyes reminded him of a time during the War; a friend of his had been ripped open by shell fire and lay painfully wounded in the slime at the bottom of a trench, his intestines bobbing in the muddy water. Sam saw the agony in his friend's eyes and shot him to put him out of his misery. It hadn't been this painful.

She twisted her hands free, and with a last look, tears flowing, jaw flexing, she turned and headed for the stern on legs that felt rubbery.

Sam took a deep breath, then turned away from her to hide the pain in his own face, hide an expression that showed his heart was broken, too. Maybe more than hers.

Linda retook her spot close to Tom, sniffing and wiping tears from her cheeks. She stomped her feet on the deck in an angry little jig, mad at herself for falling in love, for giving her heart and trusting him.

Tom, head down, feigning sleep, tried to keep from laughing. He had heard everything. It had exceeded his wildest expectations. What a show! Now he could get her out of this hellhole and back to New York—then catch her on the rebound. Brilliant. The delicious taste of victory suddenly flooded him.

No one noticed the engine sound of a small plane that droned in the sky above them. A small, silver float plane with a World Rubber logo painted on it was winging its way over the jungle.

· · · · ● · ● ● · · ·

The chairman and lawyer number one sat in the small interior of the plane, going over papers.

"About time we heard from Jackman," remarked the chairman.

"What do you expect? If he's willing to play her for a sucker, he'll double cross us too. It's dangerous," replied the lawyer.

"She's a pain in the ass and so is he. I wish they'd all disappear in the jungle. Hey, pilot, how much longer?"

J.J. leaned his head into the cabin. "Hard to say—couple of hours...got to stay flexible."

•••••••••••

The mail boat slid up to the Iquitos dock past J.J.'s anchored float plane.

The Sampan Saloon was visible in the background as Sam stumbled down the gangway, while behind, Tom helped Linda. Sam turned back to see her once more, but people pushed between them, and he turned away and headed for the saloon.

Linda watched him go into the bar, confused and empty. She was biting her thumbnail, trying to decide what to do.

Tom tried to distract her. "Well, there's the plane, darling. I know how this whole rotten misadventure must have upset you, but believe me, once we're back in New York, you'll forget this entire escapade and we can—"

She cut him off, "I told you, I'm not going back."

"What?" Tom was incredulous. "After all that's happened? Surely you can't expect me to—"

"I don't expect you to do anything. And you better not expect anything of me." She shouted through angry tears, "When are you, or Sam, or Truman, for that matter, going to learn that a woman is a person too? I have my own dreams, my own life to live and I'm going to live it without your permission...without anyone's permission."

"But, but what about the plane?"

"You take it," she retorted over her shoulder as she started away.

"Where are you going? What will you do?" he called after her.

"Wire a bank, scrape up some money—hire a guide—buy supplies."

Tom watched helplessly as she stalked away, losing herself in the dock crowd.

• • • ● • ● • • •

Tom hustled to the World Rubber Office building, where he was surprised to find a car waiting, and more surprised to have the car take him out of town. They passed the city squalor and drove into the back country, through a guarded, grilled iron gate, to a private road lined with mansions, all surrounded by beautified jungle.

The car swung into a long driveway and stopped in front of a Spanish colonial two-story which Tom assumed belonged to Truman.

Ushered in by a silent butler, he was taken through the home to a rear patio, where the chairman and his lawyer sat at a table, drinking from ice filled glasses.

The chairman smiled, "Hiya, Tom, sit down, wanna a drink?" Then looking around, "Where's Mrs. Dawson?"

Tom sat heavily and told them everything, ending with, "She went to buy supplies."

He slumped in his chair, trembling slightly from tiredness and a growing anxiety about the future. The Chairman digested the story. It didn't make him happy.

"Where is she now?"

"I'm not sure," Tom shrugged helplessly. "I'd like to take a hot shower, get cleaned up."

"Not yet. Hey, you, bring me a phone!"

"Can I get a drink?" asked Tom as the butler brought a phone on a long cord and the chairman dialed.

"In a minute. Hello, Johnson? Look, we've got a problem and I'm counting on your help. This has to happen fast!" The chairman explained what he wanted and hung up.

"Look, I've been in these clothes for days. I could use a shower."

"Not now—you have to get going."

"What?"

"She said she's going on, right?"

Tom nodded, saw the bullet coming in slow motion.

The chairman stood and placed a hand on Tom's shoulder, "Well, we have to have someone go with her."

"Oh, no, not me," Tom said, wagging his finger, suddenly feeling the tremors returning. "She'll get me killed." Then in a more imploring tone, "You don't know what it's like out there."

The chairman saw weakness in Tom's eyes, fear even, but went on as if he hadn't, "It has to be you, my boy," he said, patting Tom's shoulder, "you're the only one she trusts."

One of the chairman's lawyers, sitting quietly until now, watching Tom through beady eyes, darted in like a barracuda, "She does still trust you, doesn't she? Otherwise maybe we should find someone else." He finished by looking to the chairman, who pursed his lips and tilted his head thoughtfully.

Tom was caught and he knew it. Suddenly, he hated everything. He hated his lawyerly ambition, hated the Amazon, hated the idea of going back into that green hell, spending more uncomfortable hours, days, weeks, out of his element, fearing for his life every second. He even hated Linda, that silly, stupid woman, bringing him down here and then ignoring his advice. He hated the chairman and all his double-dealing, back-stabbing lawyers who were now patronizing him and sending him to his death with a wink and a nod.

But he was stuck. If he quit now and Linda was killed, he'd lose everything. If she found Truman, his hiding the letter would be exposed...and he'd get nothing. If Sam came back into the picture...he'd get nothing. If she found the treasure alone...he'd get nothing. If he wanted any kind of pay-off, he had to go.

"Alright," was all he said, quietly dying inside, staring into empty space, feeling bile rising in his stomach.

They all saw a change in Tom's countenance. Something had ebbed away. When he finally looked up and met the chairman's eyes, he looked faded, older. His nervous animation was gone.

The chairman became uncomfortable under Tom's dead stare. "Good, it's settled, here's some money, get yourself something to wear in town."

He looked at his pocket watch to avoid Tom's eyes. "Well, well, look at the time. We must be going. I want to have dinner in Rio, perhaps take in a show. I hear those Samba girls are really something," he said, nudging Tom and smiling, rubbing it in. "Come on, we'll drop you at the office. Well, come on."

Tom stood, zombie-like, wavering a little. The chairman shook Tom's hand and was surprised to find the grip strong, but the hand cold and clammy.

• • • • ● • ● • • •

Soon, Tom was standing in Johnson's office. Johnson was speaking, but Tom couldn't hear him, his head was filled with angry voices, disjointed, screaming.

"Well?" asked Johnson.

Tom came slightly awake to Johnson's voice. He nodded numbly.

Johnson went on, "...as far as your safety goes. The company will provide you with our most experienced guide. Very reliable should you...find anything you can't deal with. Want to meet him?" he said casually.

"Who?" asked Tom, his mind spinning ineffectually.

"Your guide, of course. He's right outside."

Tom nodded dully and Johnson hit the intercom. "Send him in, will you?"

A side door opened and a menacing looking, Carascas, entered. Tom noticed the ugly red facial scar from a bullet wound and knew everything he had to about the figure in front of him. The man was a killer.

Carascas smiled his gold-toothed smile and extended his hand. He saw the dead stare in Tom's eyes and knew at once that the gringo was going mad.

• • • • ● • ● • • •

Ramshackle warehouses and assorted vendor stalls lined one of the smaller, tree-lined quays that invaded the city.

Linda bought supplies and stuffed them into Truman's ruck-sack, while followed by a crowd of admiring boys. She reacted with surprise as she saw Tom enter.

"Ahh, Linda. At last. I've been looking everywhere for you."

"Forget it, Tom, I'm not changing my mind."

"Listen to me!" he demanded, surprising her with his tone, "Look, I thought about what you said. I went to the main office and told them to help you or I'd, I'd do something...in the end they agreed with me, I'll help you mount a real expedition."

"What?"

"The men are waiting outside," he nodded his head, "We have provisions, porters, and a guide. A real guide this time—a sober one."

Linda walked past him, stepped from the warehouse to a narrow landing and saw a small, steam-driven, river boat loaded with supplies. Carascas stood on board, with a half-dozen other river pirates, all smiling. He swept off his battered, straw hat. "*Tanto gusto, señora...* welcome to my country," he said, flashing his gold teeth.

Linda sensed something wrong with Tom, he was different. He had been sullen and withdrawn on much of their trip, but now—what was it? Was he sick? "Sorry Tom," she said, still trying to decipher his mood. "This is good of you, thanks."

"That's alright. We started together and we'll finish together." Tom smiled at her with his mouth, but his eyes were cold.

Linda was troubled at Tom's difference, but quickly put it aside. "Give me a moment, will you?" she said, "I have one last thing to do." She turned and briskly walked down the quay.

• • • ● •● • ● • •• •

Sam sat at a table in the Sampan Saloon. A bottle in front of him and the local tart, Carmen, sitting next to him, her arm looped with his. He looked up at the sound of the World Rubber float plane's engine wheezing and coughing to life. *It'll be over in a few minutes*, he thought, *and she'll be gone forever – good*! He poured another sloppy drink, lifted it to his lips and saw her.

Linda entered through the broken shuttered half-doors, looked around until her eyes found him, then she marched straight to his table through a crowd of gawking onlookers. She stopped and stood over him, hands on her hips, saying nothing, just looking, her jaw flexing. He wilted under her gaze.

Carmen wiggled uncomfortably as Linda tapped her on the shoulder. Carmen looked up, batting her whisk-broom eye lashes.

"Hit the freaking road, sister," Linda said, balling her fist and jerking her thumb toward the bar. Her voice so pregnant with violence that a deep hush fell over the bar and a little bet money changed hands.

Carman turned to Sam, said in a pouty voice, "Sam?"

He looked down.

Linda leaned closer, "Now, sweetheart!"

Carmen eased her chair back, legs squeaking across the wooden floor—and left.

"I just wanted to tell you that we're leaving."

"Have a nice trip," he said, not wanting to look at her anymore, hearing the plane's engines gunning.

"Damn it, Sam." Linda said, anger rising, "Why are you doing this? We could have it all if you'd just stop feeling sorry for yourself and get your nose out of that bottle."

"Awww, what do you know about it?" he said angrily, banging his fist on the table and making the glassware jump. "Big city rich girl with some fancy Paris education—slumming around the jungle, looking for a little adventure so you can go back and impress your socialite friends in New York over champagne cocktails."

They spent a moment staring at each other, him getting the worst of it.

"What do I know about it?" she started, "...what the hell do you know about anything? I've been paying my own way as long as I can remember, and my fancy education was a chorus line at the Follies, but it did teach me one thing. You've got to fight for your dreams and not drink them under the table."

Linda scooped up Sam's glass—threw her head back and tossed off the shot—did a can-can YELP as she threw a kick high over her head...then turned and strode away, to the cheers of the riff-raff crowd.

Sam was shocked. Outside, the plane's engines roared with a throaty mechanical purr. He stood from the table and wobbled to the bar entrance, where he hung on the shuttered doors. He watched the plane pull away, believing Linda to be on it, not realizing that she stood three feet away, leaning against the outside wall, waiting for him to follow her out.

The plane skip-bounced away, then took to the sky like a giant silver bird and Sam's shoulders dropped. His hand went to his head. He had just made the biggest mistake of his life and he knew it. There was nothing to do now but finish getting drunk.

A few feet away, Linda's face hardened as she dabbed her cheek and walked the other way, filled with determination to succeed, and to forget him.

She soon joined Tom and the men. "Alright then... let's go." She said, climbing aboard the launch.

"*Bueno, muchachos, vamanos*!" yelled Carascas. And they pushed off.

The little expedition floated down the quay, chugging and belching puffs of gray wood-smoke - past the eyes of traders, Indians, soldiers...and big Jim Ives.

Chapter 18

Saturday nights at the Sampan Saloon were always raucous alcohol fueled affairs. Patrons yelled and screamed as Jim Ives and another big man arm wrestled at a table. Sweat glistened in the oil lamp light as the two men grunted and strained, muscles quivering, surrounded by a screaming, money waving crowd.

A sudden pull, and Ives was thrown from the table. Jerked from his chair, He staggered drunkenly through the crowd and crashed to the floor among the legs of a distant table. The crowd cheered the winner on to another match and more bet money changed hands. Jim, forgotten, grunted, and passed out on the beer puddled floor.

• • • • • • • • • •

Morning's early rays filtered across the barroom, sparkling through dirty glasses and near-empty bottles. The janitor ran his push-broom into Jim's side stopping his fitful snoring as it woke him. Hungover and disoriented, he crawled on wet hands and knees towards the door, when he saw a dead body in the corner. Curious, Jim made his way to the recumbent form to find it was Sam, and that he was alive.

"Laddie!" he cried, shaking the body.

Sam groaned, fumbled his words, "I'm a little drunk pal, I'm just going to stand here awhile and take it easy." The janitor's push-broom made itself realized against Sam's head. "Hey," Sam said, looking through half closed eyes, "Jimmy, is that you? What are you doing here? Where are we?"

. . . . ● . ● . . .

They sat together at a small table in an open-air dive under a corrugated tin roof, eating a meal of beans and rice and meat of an undisclosed origin. Sam told Jim the whole story, finishing with, "Then like a dumb school kid, I got so sorry-ass drunk I let her get away on that plane." He took a swallow of coffee, "Hell, she's better off anyway...."

Jim slowly put the pieces together, "She's not on any plane, boyo," his big hand shaking Sam's arm, "she's gone up-river."

"What? What are you talking about?" Jim's nonsense revelation banged the thought-walls inside Sam's aching head.

"I saw her today...er, yesterday. Can't be another looker like that in town. She was headed upriver with Carascas and some bloke posturing like admiral god-damn Perry."

"That's got to be Jackman, the lawyer," said Sam, his hand brushing back his hair, trying to think clearly. "But why's Carascas with them?"

"Say, laddie, there's something foul about all this. Several weeks ago someone brought me a letter addressed to Tom Jackman at World Rubber."

"What'd you do with it?"

"Why, I turned it over to their office for a little drink money."

"You read it?"

"Well, it was kinda open."

"And?"

"It was written in a childish scrawl, a fevered hand perhaps. It said something like...not returning...give all to wife, signed, T...something or other."

"Truman? Truman Dawson?"

"Could have been. At the time I thought it was just some poor soap-dodger out croaking in the bush."

"Makes no sense, Jim. She never got that letter.... They're holding out on her." Sam stared into space, thinking.

"Well then," Jim said, "we better get going, they only have a day's head start." He started to stand, wobbled, sat.

Sam smiled as he caught Jim's arm, "I'm going alone."

"What? Why? You'll be outnumbered."

"I gotta travel fast and loose—I'll figure something out when I catch them."

"How will you find them? They could have taken the Ucayali or the Marano, or any one of a dozen tributaries."

"I know where they're going," he said darkly.

"It's that place, isn't it? The place that bit you?"

Sam nodded.

"Are you sure you can face that place again, alone?"

"For her?" He realized how deeply he loved her. "You bet."

They regarded each other a moment. Jim saw a clarity in Sam's eyes he had always missed before. "Well, maybe it's all true, about the treasure I mean. Think about it laddie, the treasure, and the girl too. What a haul boyo, what a haul. Now, how about one for the road then?" Jim raised his hand for the waiter.

Sam waved him away, "Never again, pal."

"Good for you, laddie, good for you," the big Irishman's hand shook Sam's arm as he smiled. "May the road be kind to you, Sam, and your prayers be answered."

• • • • • • • • • •

Linda's boat spent days chugging slowly up-river; and nights, unable to navigate in the dark, tied to whatever trees were available. She would consult Truman's map in secret, sometimes in the ship's only cabin, at night by candle-light—the only place where she could try and sleep in relative safety. The trip was lonely now. No Sam, only Tom—always quiet, morosely dark and withdrawn.

The loneliness ached. Chugging endlessly up the green expanse, she felt a growing dislike for the harmful looking crew. They would spend their time entertaining themselves, singing and playing reedy Andean flutes, keeping rhythm by foot stamping on the deck. Then leer at her, their eyes making their intentions obvious, speaking quietly, and laughing obscenely when she passed.

She longed for Sam. There was no getting around it. She still loved him in spite of everything.

Sometimes she felt near collapse, struggling to maintain her sanity as the ceaseless repetitive throbbing of the engine beat against her brain. Watching the thick green foliage float past, clammy with sweat in the humidity, she began to feel entombed in the jungle. She found it ironic that from a distance, the jungle looked like the Garden of Eden, up close it was as rotten with death as Devil's Island.

Tom had spent the days trying to plan for various scenarios. He could see that these men the company had given him were the dregs of society, and that was saying a lot considering the society they were in was a product of the most dangerous jungle in the world. He knew the company didn't care about Linda, or him—this meant that his life was on the line also, and he had no one to look to for help expect himself.

All this meant one thing. In order to survive he had to be the most ruthless, most cunning, most dangerous person on this trip, be willing to sacrifice and kill. Yes...murder, if need be, to survive.

His fear pumped adrenaline into his system allowing him to stay awake for long periods. He would sit in silence, his back to the cabin wall, hand always hovering close to his pistol, watching the men through hollow, red-rimmed eyes, alert for any sign of danger in their expressions, tone of voice or looks.

After days of this, even the headhunters became uncomfortable around him. Only Carascas was unconcerned. He understood. He felt the same way.

• • • ● • ● • • •

The monotony was broken, when Linda sighted the few huts that constituted a barley civilized outpost, and recognizing this was a reference point, she directed the ship's captain to turn off the Rio Marano onto the Huallaga.

This was the moment Carascas had waited for. Now he knew where they were headed, and he knew what the old Gringo he had been chasing had been after—treasure. The thought had him recalculate his plans, maybe he wouldn't kill the Americans too soon, as the rubber company had hinted.

They changed from the steam launch to canoes to continue their trip up a narrowing tributary that rose between steep-sided foothills into the mountains.

The watercourse became narrow and swift, and they had to halt more and more frequently to carry their boats and supplies past impassable rapids or around waterfalls. It became colder too, as the sun penetrated into the deep valleys less and less.

After a few days, they landed when they clearly heard the rushing sound of a large waterfall.

With Carascas giving orders, the men began unloading their supplies at the edge of the blackened and overgrown remains of an abandoned village.

"I wonder what happened here?" Linda asked.

Carascas shrugged, remembering having raided this same place months before. "The back-country, you know, very dangerous," he smiled, wiping his sweaty forehead with a dirty coat sleeve.

Linda continued searching through the charred destruction while the men shouldered the supplies and prepared to trail out. Even now the jungle was reclaiming the site, with grass and vines almost having consumed the former dwellings; yet here and there bones could be seen littering the ground. *What a murderous place to live,* she thought.

"Alright, come-on, we're ready to go," came Tom's voice, gruffer and more commanding than she remembered.

They started up a muddy track that left the village and headed into the grey fog that blurred the greenery and shrouded the mountains above. The only sounds were bird calls, monkey chatter and machetes hacking brush.

• • • • • • • • • •

No longer friendly with the river police, since his reputation for losing a detachment of soldiers now followed him, Sam had hitched a ride on a river supply boat. When he reached the small settlement at the Huallaga, he debarked and bought himself a canoe. Soon he was paddling upstream in the narrowing, dark channel.

He knew he could catch them, that wasn't the problem, the problem would be how to approach them. Carascas would be armed and dangerous, that much he knew. The rest—he'd have to see and play it by ear.

The solitude of his journey gave him time to think about his ayahuasca dream...what it had revealed to him. It showed him that his former, drunken, daredevil courage, had been based on his contempt for death. A contempt that was generated by his own feeling of unworthiness—his life didn't matter to him, so it had been easy to act recklessly. Now it was reversed, now he cared about his life because he loved Linda, and that made him see things differently, things he would have never considered before, like staying alive, like the future. Maybe a future with her. Now his courage would be strengthened by love; and it made him felt better.

When he reached the waterfall village, he beached his canoe, and shouldered his rucksack. Then stared up into the wild tangle of jungle that gradually faded into the looming mountains.

"Okay then," he said to himself, "here goes nothing." And he plunged into the wet greenery, quickly finding and following their trail.

· • • ● • ● • • ·

Linda and her party spent the better part of a week tortuous climbing and chopping trail up the steep muddy slopes, until finally, they reached the summit of a tree covered ridge, where they stopped to rest.

Linda's face was dirty and wet with perspiration, as she gained the flat ground. Breathing heavily, she saw a line of human skulls, suspended high above them, hoisted aloft on long bamboo poles. She had caught glimpses of these white floating things from time to time during their climb, but thought they might be birds or flowers, nesting high in the distant trees. Now they grinned down at her in their macabre silence, with only the thin whistle of the wind that animated them.

She turned at the murmuring she heard behind her and saw the porters looking jittery and nervous.

Below them, they saw a long narrow valley, winding snake like, to be lost in the distant haze among the fog-shrouded peaks.

Tom pushed his way next to her and looked up to see the grim line of silent sentinels. "Well," he said, "looks like the end of the line—for them anyway."

Carascas explained, "Some kind of Indian sign—maybe they don't want no-one to go this way." He remembered the place.. .remembered the last time he had been in the valley. For the first time in many years, he crossed himself. "We better go down and find a place to camp. The men don't want to stay up here."

They hadn't gone far when a sudden shot from behind stopped them. They turned to see Carascas stone faced, gun in hand.

"What's going on?" yelled Linda.

"The Indians, superstitious. You know. They try to run away." Carascas shrugged as he stuck his pistol back into the waistband of his pants.

"So, you're going to shoot them?"

"Come on, Linda," said Tom, mopping his forehead with a wet handkerchief, "Let's go. They're his men." He took her roughly by the arm and pulled her along.

Linda thought Tom's eyes looked red-rimmed and glassy. She had been noticing how Tom's attitude had changed since they had started out from Iquitos. *He must have a fever or something,* she thought, feeling more alone than ever.

They slipped and skidded down the steep muddy track until they reached the valley floor. It was swampy, with a few higher and drier places to pitch camp. They found a spot among a grove of tall trees where they strung their hammocks. The men off-loaded their burdens and rubbed the stiffness from their shoulders.

Soon a fire was going, and they stayed within its illuminated reach, as everything outside that flickering yellow was quickly swallowed by inky shadows.

Different animal noises began at sunset. Night's denizens grunted and growled in unfamiliar voices, sounding closer and more dangerous than the party was used to from the lowlands.

Linda lay in her hammock, catching intermittent views of the deep indigo sky through the swaying branches, and tried to relax, seeing high above, the usual stars burning in comforting familiarity. She reflected on how these highlands were quite different from the lowland jungle she had traversed the last few weeks. First, the smell—up here it was heavy with rotten fruit, stagnant water, and animal musk, all sickly and putrid; and the sounds—below were people...people the animals were familiar with, and shy of. Here there was no-one, and the animals shouted their contempt and anger from the brush—unafraid.

She was afraid, afraid and worried about Tom. He had been acting more and more strange since leaving Iquitos. Now she was sure he had contracted some kind of sickness. She had seen his appetite wane, and watched him as he had grown thinner; now his face was gaunt, almost skeletal. She knew that the energy required by his exertion had consumed his available fat and was now eating into his muscle fiber, causing his perspiration to smell bitter and ammonia like. Still, he seemed to have plenty of nervous energy, scanning the surroundings with quick, animal-like darting glances through red-rimmed eyes.

What if anything should happen to him? she wondered, not daring to imagine her fate if left alone with Carascas and his crew.

Her thoughts went to Sam. *How is he?* she wondered, *where was he? And why had he acted the way he did? To send her home, to save her?*

She wasn't mad at him anymore, just sad, and curious as to why he treated her the way he had. She wished more than ever he was with her right now. Oddly she felt as though he was close, that somehow, he was still protecting her, watching over her—of course, she knew that was silly.

She closed her eyes and drifted into the heavy sleep of the thoroughly exhausted.

Chapter 19

S am sat on the ridge above Linda's camp. Above him, the mounted skulls bobbed and swayed, a grim reminder, etched in the memory of his last time here. His stomach felt uneasy.

He saw the pinpoint of yellow light below that marked their campfire and decided to wait until morning to make his move. That left him alone with the swaying skulls for the night.

The valley of death, he thought as he settled onto his ground-cloth. *What an apt name.* He remembered the poem called, "The Charge of the Light Brigade", an ode to a famous vain-glorious, suicidal cavalry charge that ended in destruction for so many. "Into the valley of death rode the six hundred," was the line that came to mind. Not a morale building thought.

Then he remembered another reference to a different valley of death, "Yea, though I walk through the valley of death, I shall fear no evil, thy rod, and thy staff, they comfort me...surely goodness shall follow me all the days of my life..." He shook his head. It had been a long time since he had thought of those words, funny he should think of them now. Maybe not so funny.

He looked up at the stars, immovable, eternal. And thinking of Linda, and their shared love, he passed into the arms of Morpheus.

· · · · ● · ● · · · ·

Linda woke the next morning to the sounds of trees groaning and creaking, their highest branches being pushed by a morning breeze. These uplands were cooler than the country below, and the crispness of the early grey light, brought a chill with it. She swung her feet to the forest floor as she shivered. The men would be up soon and asking for directions. Before they started peppering her with questions, she would consult Truman's map again—as always, in secret.

The sun was rising quickly, clearing the ridge line above them, sending slender shafts to penetrate the canopy and dapple the forest floor. She wandered away from camp in the direction of the first yellow patches of scattered sunlight.

Finding a flat stone among the foliage, she withdrew Truman's map from her secret bank envelope, carefully spreading the ancient cartographer's work on the moss-covered surface, thankful that the sun was providing a little warmth with its emerging light.

The old ink lines were sepia and vague, but she scrutinized them, recognizing terrain references, and it seemed that she had arrived, at least generally, at the place marked with an X. Was this it? There didn't seem to be anything here.

Had it all been for nothing? She released a sigh, and bit her thumb nail, trying to think, trying to fortify herself against the growing sense of disappointment.

She scanned her surroundings absentmindedly. The shafts of light, steadily creeping into the forest, revealed more and more detail, abstracting shapes from the pervading gloom.

Then she saw a glint of something, then another. And as she watched with growing wonder, a jumble of stones arose from the surrounding shadows. She realized that even the stone where she had laid her map was a smooth cut one, shaped by human hands. She realized, almost weak with a strange giddiness, that she had discovered, El Dorado, the fabled lost treasure city of the Amazons.

"Tom, Tom," she called a bit breathless, "Come quick, hurry!"

· · · ● · ● ● · · ·

Sam watched from above through his field glasses. He had stayed back on purpose, not wanting to tangle with Carascas and his men during the thicker part of their ascending trek. The valley floor would be the place to do it, offering more room for mobility and line-of-sight shooting, with fewer places to get ambushed. It might all go peacefully, then again, maybe not. That's also why he had tried to stay upwind of Linda's party, which was sure to have some old native tracker capable of smelling him out.

Standing from cover, he let the glasses drop to his chest as he readied himself to go down-trail; now, when the sun rose behind him and would be in their eyes.

Sam could feel a slight tightening in his chest as he reflexively checked his kit, sliding his hand over the large hunting knife on his ammunition belt, then the holster with his big 45. Caliber revolver. He inspected his Winchester shot-gun, great at short range, like the trench-gun he had used many times while with the Marines. To support everything, his rucksack carried extra ammunition and a first-aid kit.

· · · · ● · ● · · · ·

Linda and Tom stood with Carascas and the others surveying the panorama of ruins that drifted away from sight into the thick foliage and dark shadows. The sight of the tumbled stone walls inspired a kind of respectful quietude. The morning sounds of bird calls and monkey jabber seemed a fitting welcome.

"I wonder how old this pace is," she asked quietly, more to herself than anyone else.

She led Tom and the others into the overgrown rubble. Behind, the native porters looked apprehensive.

"Linda, we've found it," said Tom, amazement softening his features.

There was a long low rumbling growl, then another, like something big and dangerous waking up; but they all were too excited by their discovery to be alarmed.

Linda was entranced by the ruins. The sky lightened to a pale blue, and the light was general but soft. Steamy vapor rose in ground fog, as if to hide the silent stones, and blur her view; but she pressed forward, drawn deeper into the mysterious overgrown city.

Tom found Linda looking at the smiling face of an overturned statue; unknowingly, the same one that Sam had used for his demonstration.

"Look!" she said. "This looks like the little statue I found on Truman's desk...the thing that started all of this."

Tom looked around, had they really found the fabled city? Was there a real treasure to uncover? His mind began to work on the possibilities. He watched Linda pick her way through the middle distance, childlike in her wonder, innocent. What a fool. She couldn't be trusted to share it, not really. What would happen if they did find Inca gold? Truman was dead, he had to be. That left her... What would happen if an accident befell her? Who would know? Who could find out? And what about Carascas? He definitely couldn't be trusted unless he was guaranteed a share. Even then he probably would have ambitions to kill both of them and keep the gold for himself. No, Carascas would have to go too. And, of course, back in Iquitos there was that bother, Sam. Sam could be counted on to intrude in some way. And should Sam and Linda start talking, they might discover his own duplicity. So many things to worry about. Loose ends, there were always loose ends.

Carascas approached and motioned to Tom, and the two stepped well out of her earshot. "Someone's following us..." hissed Carascas conspiratorially, "Sam Black I think."

At the mention of Sam's name, Tom became furious. This had to be the last time he would ever have to contend with Sam. "You know him?" growled Tom.

Carascas, was surprised at the malevolence in Tom's voice as he rubbed the facial scar Sam's bullet had given him, "I know him, but we ain't friends."

Tom looked to see if Linda was listening. Satisfied she wasn't, he leaned closer to Carascas, and clutching his arm, said simply, "Kill him."Carascas, smiled, "Better if you go on. I want to settle a score with him anyway, if I catch him alive it'll take some time."

This could be the answer to everything, Tom thought, *get them to kill each other, and I'll deal with Linda.*

Tom nodded and watched Carascas lead the others back towards camp, then hurried to catch up with Linda, "We should go to the end of the ruins," he said, "see how far they extend."

"But there's so much to see right here."

"I know, but they're everywhere. We can search more diligently on our walk back."

Another low growl grunted from the brush.

"Did you hear that?" she looked around. "What do you suppose that was?"

"Don't know." He patted his pistol confidently, "Don't worry, whatever it is, I'll kill it." He said with ghoulish delight. His deathly grin unnerved her.

Tom and Linda soon found a roadway, disrupted by the trees that had grown through the paving-stones. It seemed to lead away towards the center of the mysterious ruins, and they followed it between the tumbled walls that squatted in the dappled sunlight. As they got deeper into the ruins, the had to hack their way through the dense foliage that had grown under the canopy of trees. Linda became more and more excited, wondering what they might discover, wondering if they would really find ancient Inca treasure.

Finally, they came to the remains of a stone portico, a broad pillared porch that fronted a large structure. They stopped in amazement, sharing a look. The sounds of buzzing insects filled the hot, humid air, while bird cries and monkey screeches screamed warnings from the temple's inhabitants.

The humidity rose and the familiar feel of perspiration covered Linda's face and soaked her clothing as she mounted the crumbling steps and walked through the arched entrance.

Once inside, Linda and Tom stood facing a large plaza, now almost unrecognizable under the heavy undergrowth. And ahead, on the other side, a stone pavilion raised two stories into the dank air, laying wrecked by creeping vines and tree roots, covered by centuries of jungle growth; sections overturned and scattered in rubble.

"Must be a palace of some kind," offered Tom, with uncharacteristic giddiness, his own mind racing feverishly at the nearing possibility of discovering some fabulously wealthy treasure. He had noticed the golden objects, some encrusted with emeralds, at the museum; but not given them serious thought. Now, everything might have changed. Now he might be richer than his wildest fantasies. If they found any treasure, it would be his and his alone. He'd see to that.

As they climbed the steps to the building, Linda saw the unhealthy glint in Tom's eyes and attributed it to his sickness.

How long, she wondered, *how long before he cracks-up, dies, goes mad? What will I do then?"* The thought made her swallow hard.

They entered the palace under a stepped stone arch, finding the general clammy darkness broken only in places by the narrow shafts of light that stabbed through missing pieces of stonework. They continued advancing cautiously through the connected anterooms, under the colonies of sleeping bats that hung from the ceiling, all while listening for the unexpected, for other things might be living there, waking to their echoing footsteps that disturbed the silence of centuries.

Finally, they pushed their way through giant webs and found themselves in a large space. The ceiling had collapsed in various places, offering more filtered light and strewn rubble across the floor. They could tell it had been a throne room by the dais and large carved throne that stood at one end of the great hall.

They separated, each exploring the surrounding edges for openings, other rooms that might have been for treasure storage.

They finally met back at the throne room, disappointment etched into their faces.

Linda sat on the dais. "Well, I guess there's no treasure after all." She said bleakly.

But Tom wasn't listening, he was staring up into the throne itself. Linda followed his gaze – and realized that the dark crumpled shape they thought was a mass of fallen vegetation, was the remains of a person.

She quickly stood. One word escaped her mouth—"Truman?"

There, above them, sat a decomposing skeleton, still wrapped in a rotten Indian blanket, sightless eye sockets aimed at its broken surroundings, mouth agape in silent laughter.

"My God," uttered Tom.

Chapter 20

S am had dodged off the trail when he saw some of the Indian porters running away.

That'll even things up a bit, he thought, deciding to wait to make an entrance until the porters had enough time to get clear, and not return to fight against him. He looked again through his field-glasses, watching Carascas deploy his remaining men in ambush.

Carascas, waited behind a large tree, concealed by low shrubbery and shadows, from where he could watch the trail coming down from the skull festooned ridge. All was quiet except for the soft sound of the tall swamp grass being moved by a gentle wind, and the ever-present dull hum of insect clouds. He had arranged his men in a crude semi-circle with overlapping fields of view, and now they waited for Sam in silence.

One of his men had a blowgun to his mouth, the other end, resting in the fork of a tree, pointed to a clearing just ahead.

Suddenly, Sam's rifle butt swung out of the darkness and hit the muzzle of the blowgun, driving the near end through the head of the waiting bandit.

Men yelled and gunfire exploded, as the two sides tried to kill each other. Sam, hardened to this kind of fighting in the Marines, rolled through the brush dodging bullets, only to stand and fire on a close target with his shotgun.

Linda turned to the muffled sounds of gunfire coming from camp. "What's that? What's going on?" she asked Tom.

"Probably the men doing some hunting," he said in return.

But Linda grew more intent, straining to hear the dimly echoing reports. "That's not hunting," she said, "That's a gunfight."

"Don't be silly."

"Listen. Hear it? That's a shotgun! None of our men had shotguns." Her face blanched as she realized that it had to be Sam. "I'm going back," she shouted as she turned and started through the doorway and outside.

Once in the stone plaza she heard Tom, behind her, yell, "Stop!"

She paused at the stone arch and looked back. She could see that Tom was holding his pistol on her.

"Stay where you are!" he demanded.

"Tom!?"

"Just stay where you are, or I'll shoot." He thumbed the hammer back on his revolver.

Linda, assailed by confusion, shouted, "Don't you understand? Sam, it's Sam! And Carascas is trying to kill him."

"Never mind that," Tom said stepping forward, his voice rough, his face a mask of evil intent. "We'll know what's happened soon enough. Just sit down." He motioned with his pistol.

"Tom...." Her voice, full of disappointment tinged with anger at the realization of his duplicity.

"Keep quiet," he said, keeping his pistol trained on her while checking their back-trail. "I'm prepared to shoot, even you, if I have to."

• • • • • • • • • •

Carascas and Sam stood facing each other, alone. Both men were breathing heavily. Everyone else was either dead or dying, or had vanished into the brush.

Sam leveled his shotgun at Carascas, who raised his pistol and pulled the trigger. The dull metallic click telling both men the pistol was empty. Carascas, threw the gun at Sam, who dodged, then defiantly, spit in Sam's direction. Sam lay his shotgun down, and staring at Carascas, drew his knife and dropped his gun-belt. Carascas smiled at the challenge and drew a knife of his own, grinning.

The two men circled each other warily, then came together in a vicious, hand to hand struggle. They stumbled over fallen logs and stone walls, slashing, and stabbing at each other—Carascas was bigger, but Sam was quicker, and soon both men had drawn blood. Wheezing and gasping for breath, they tumbled over giant tree roots, finally splashing into a dark, stagnant swamp that smelled of decay and death.

They grappled, slipping on the slick muddy bottom, until Sam grabbed Carascas by the neck and shoved him into the deep shadows—which exploded with blood and foam as giant croco-dile jaws ripped from the water and tore a screaming Carascas in half. Sam froze. Around him, large yellow eyes blinked from the shadows. At once Sam realized what had happened to Castillo and his men. Up here, away from natural predators, the crocks had grown to enormous size. That's why the skulls sat atop the ridge, a warning sign not to enter.

Tom, and Linda, heard a distant scream, too plaintive to be human, too human to be anything else. Linda shuddered, and sat heavily on a broken wall. "Why, Tom? Why?"

"Let's just wait a little and see who survived. After all, we don't want to rush into anything too dangerous. Do we?"

They waited, both filled with nervous anticipation for differ-ent reasons. Linda fidgeted, tormented, and frustrated at the thought of Sam being hurt out there somewhere and needing help, and her not being able to leave. Tom hovered over her, his pistol tapping her shoulder as a reminder, restraining her as he watched the jungle with unflinching alertness.

Minutes ticked by. The sun rose higher. No one came. The jungle returned to normal, with monkey babbling and bird hooting. The heat and humidity became oppressive-still they waited, surrounded by the broken stones of a long dead city.

Tom regarded Linda, "Well," he said, "It looks like it's just you and me now."

"Tom, what's gotten into you? What have you done?" she pleaded.

"Done? I've assumed my rightful place, that's all," he snarled. "I've always been the superior person. You just forgot it. Now, let's talk about us, shall we?"

"There is no 'us'," she said with contempt. "I'm going back, Sam might be hurt." She started to stand.

Tom grabbed Linda. Pulled her close. She tore herself free, stared at him defiantly. His mood turned darker. He hit her hard enough to send her to the ground, then stood over her, breath hot with excitement, beads of acrid perspiration falling from his face to hers.

"I really thought you were something special," he spit, "but you're nothing more than a little gold-digging tramp. They stared into each other's eyes. Her hate was as plain as his lust.

Then they heard Sam's voice calling, "Linda!?"

Tom looked over the rubble, and seeing Sam coming towards them, shotgun slung over his shoulder, quickly aimed his pistol. Linda sprung to her feet, shoved Tom, shouting, "Sam, look out!" Tom's pistol exploded and Sam fell.

Linda grabbed Tom, shaking him, "You fool, we'll never get out of here alive without him!"

Tom paused, maybe she was right. He motioned with his pistol for her to go to his body. Linda rushed to Sam's side with Tom close behind, still prepared to squeeze off another shot.

She found Sam off the side of the cobble-stone road, his breath rising and falling under his bloody shirt. Linda quickly found the bullet wound. Tom's shot had grazed his side, inches from his heart, breaking a rib.

Sam gasped, "My ruck-sack, first aid kit."

His head fell back in pain. Linda searched his bag, quickly coming up with the medical supplies. Sam held his side trying to stench the flow of blood.

"Good shot, Tom, I didn't think you had it in you."

"There's a lot you never thought about." Tom smirked.

Linda cut away Sam's shirt.

"Find the sulfur powder. Pour a lot in there," he said, watching her mend him, "Hey, you're pretty good at this."

"Farm girl, remember?" she brushed blond hair from her face, "Everyone in the family fell off a combine, or a horse, or something." They smiled at each other.

"So, Tom, what now?" asked Sam.

Tom had found a close place to sit and watch, still covering them with his pistol. "I'm not too sure," he said.

"Did you ever tell her about the letter?"

"Shut up!" Tom said defensively.

"What letter?" she asked, looking from Sam to Tom.

"Go ahead, tell her. What difference can it make now?"

"Shut-up, I said."

"Your husband, Truman, left a letter, sent it to Tom here, giving everything to you, everything—everything he owned."

Linda's face went blank. She turned to Tom, "Is that true?"

Tom said nothing, his countenance growing in embarrassment.

Linda sat next to Sam, looking from Sam to Tom and back. Then smiled, then chuckled, then laughed uproariously, rocking back and forth, slapping her legs.

"What's so funny?" asked Tom, glaring at her through narrow dark-rimmed eyes, unable to understand her reaction.

Linda, tears of laughter running down her face, pointed at him, "You! You're what's so funny. Tom Jackman, the 'superior man'. Tom, honestly, you are the dumbest son-of-a-bitch on God's green earth."

Tom's expression faded. They could see his mind racing behind his eyes as he fought his confusion.

Linda leaned forward, anger building, "What do you think would have happened if you had been honest and showed me that letter?"

Tom said nothing. Suddenly feeling he had made an enormous mistake of some kind.

"I'll tell you." She went on, "I'd have taken enough money to get myself a little farm someplace and appointed you to run everything! If you had been honest with me, you'd be running World Rubber right now. Sitting in the chairman's corner office, giving orders and impressing the 'head' secretary, if you know what I mean. You would be the richest man in New York. But no! Old Tom Jackman, the 'superior person' is sitting in the middle of the freaking Amazon, broke as a church-mouse, ready to shoot the only man who can get us out alive.... Honest to God, Tom, you're the biggest fool I've ever met. You're so stupid, you're pitiful!"

She stopped and glared at him.

Tom's hand went to his forehead as he tried to get his thoughts in order. "Look, look, I was only waiting for the right moment, that's all."

He knelt between Linda and Sam, laid his pistol next to his knee and reached into his trousers, frantically searching the money belt tied around his waist. Almost instantly he came up with the soiled envelope and Truman's letter. "See? I still have it. It's not too late." He handed the letter to Linda, his mind racing to find a plan, a plausible explanation, as he tried to read her expression.

Linda took the letter out of his hand. She could see Tom's eyes twitch nervously as she unfolded the tattered missive.

"It's not too late," he choked dryly, "Look, I apologize. I know I've made a few mistakes, but now we can start over. Be partners, just like you wanted, see?"

Linda read the letter, then handed it to Sam. Sam read it and shook his head, "All this—for what?" They both stared at Tom.

Tom stood, his anger returning. "You wouldn't understand, neither of you. It was all about the leverage! The...the ability to construct a deal. The control, the manipulation! Well, I'm still in control!" He reached for his pistol. "I can kill you both and the company...." he fumbled with his waistband, searching. "...the company..."

"You looking for this?" Sam asked, holding Tom's pistol on him. "The lady's right, you are one dumb son-of-a-bitch."

Tom watched them smile at him—self-satisfied smiles, condemning smiles—and started hyperventilating.

What had happened? What had gone wrong? he wondered, starting to notice little unwanted gasps and sobs breaking from his lips. He took a mental inventory as he turned in tight little circles, combing his hair with trembling fingers. He had played it—he had played it—all wrong! He had become what he most detested, a fool! Blinded by his own feelings of superiority he had outsmarted himself. He felt laughter bubbling up inside, the laughter of the greed that had betrayed him. He dizzily collapsed, maniacal laughter slowing spilling from his lips. He knelt against a fallen stone, his head held in the crook of his arm, his free hand flexing and pounding the hard uncaring surface, trying to drive away the demons with his own pain.

They watched his sadness a while, listened to his sobbing, until they had enough.

Sam said, "I know how you feel. It happened to me too. Right over there." He waved the pistol towards the valley entrance. "Funny, it must be something about this place."

Linda wrapped her arm around Sam's shoulders. "How're you doing?" she asked.

"Okay, I guess, better than him," he nodded at the pathetic figure huddled in the stonework as he stuffed the pistol in his belt, then standing, re-shouldered his shotgun.

"You sure you're ready to go?"

"Sure," he nodded, "Let's see the ruins first, maybe we can find something."

Sam hung on Linda for support; leaving Tom to his misery, they went back into the palace.

Tom crouched against the fallen building block, watching them walk away together, seeds of revenge sprouting in his madness taking hold.

They're going to kill me. That's what I'd do in their place. They can't trust me anymore, so they'll kill me. They have the pistol and a shotgun...I have to find something.

He stood and quickly navigated the ruins to the area where he knew the ambush site to have been, and searched until he found what he was looking for—a pistol and two bullets. Giddy at the discovery, his hands wrung the pistol, *I've got to be smart –*

I've got to be smart about this. He knew that Sam was the better shot, a better woodsman. He didn't dare confront them in a fair fight. *What if I miss?* He searched the area for an ambush spot – until his eyes found Skull Ridge. *There, up there.* He reasoned that they would have to climb the steep muddy trail to leave the valley, and when they did, they would be struggling, helping each other—unprepared.

Tom scrambled up the narrow slippery track until he reached the top and found a place to conceal himself in the tall grass. Peering down-trail, he fought to catch his breath. He allowed himself a choked laugh, imagining the startled expressions on their faces when he would shoot them. *How surprised they'll be to find I've outsmarted them.* He allowed himself a small chuckle, *I still have the superior mind.* The thought comforted him as he settled into the high grass and waited, the silent skulls above him bobbed, welcoming his companionship.

· · · ● ·● ·● · ·· ·

Sam and Linda searched until they were tired, never finding any treasure. They decided to bury Truman, and when they removed the body from its resting place, they discovered a diary. Truman had chronicled his trek and personal feelings, some passages were garbled and incoherent, but there was enough to guarantee Linda's rightful claim of inheritance.

Sad and weary, they buried Linda's husband in the plaza, under a stone cairn.

When they got outside, they found Tom gone without a trace. They called and searched, but it seemed the jungle had devoured him. They finally stopped looking.

"What do you think happened to him?" she asked with resigned sadness, looking at the endless green expanse.

"The jungle," Sam shrugged, "It does funny things to people." He thought about curi-puri, the legendary primal force of reckoning, pulling the threads of behavior.

"Well," she said, "What now?"

"Hey," Sam said suddenly, "do you still have the map, Truman's map?"

"Sure, why look at it now?"

"Give it here—I might be the second dumbest person next to Tom."

Sam took the tattered map from Linda and spread it on a tumbled stone face. Soon he was laughing.

"What is it? What's so funny?"

"Look for yourself," he pointed at the faint sepia lines, his finger tracing their route from Iquitos to the valley of death. "See here? We're about three hundred miles from Iquitos to the east, but only maybe forty-fifty miles from Quito, in the west." He looked up, shaking a knife-hand towards the mountains in front of them.

"I don't understand, there's nothing marked on the map."

"Don't you see? This is a copy of a hand-drawn map made when, three, four hundred years ago? If those conquistadors had circled around from the mission, they probably didn't know where they were, or where anything else was either, but I know that city is there today," his expression shone as he looked from the distance to Linda's face.

Buoyed by his energized confidence, Linda tried to grasp Sam's revelation while he happily went on, "We don't have to go back the same way. It'll be tough going, but I still have enough ammunition to bring down some game, and I'm sure there are other little pueblos, farmers, something between us and the city."

"This town, Quito, can we get to Lima from there?"

"Sure, why?"

"Oh, I know a little place where we can stay, that's all," she said, smiling at him, thinking of them sharing a room at the hotel in Lima, eating shrimp cocktails and dancing in the moonlight.

Sam looked into her eyes, her face—God, he loved her. "You know that letter, the diary?" he said, "You're in the money now, kid. How's it feel to be the world's richest woman?"

"Who needs it?" she said, wrapping her arms around him. "Sam?" she asked, biting her thumb nail, would you like me to have your babies?"

"What? Of course," he said, kissing her...feeling her kiss him back, "lots of them."

"That's good," she smiled, "cause the first one's due in about eight months."

He beamed, "You crazy broad."

"You big lunk."

THE END

Also Written...

Other fiction written by Richard LaMotte:
A Crime Story
Halfbreeds
The Song of Ramon and Maria

Non fiction:
Costume Design 101

Visit https://RichardLaMotte.com
for information and news about upcoming books and free book
previews

About Author

Richard LaMotte loves stories. Stories about history, about people, about mysterious and exotic places, about love, danger, and adventure. Stories about behavior, about motivation, about self-realization and self-deception – in other words, stories about us - us humans.

This passion is a result of Richard joining the Marine Corp just out of high school. A passion born out of working in the motion picture industry as a costume designer, art director, technical advisor, and director – traveling around the world, setting up departments in foreign countries, working with major Hollywood actors and actresses.

Storyteller. Worked in off-beaten places in six continents. History lover. Reader and researcher. Collector. Artist. Designer. Music lover. Husband. Father. Observer of people.

Full of life's experiences, Richard LaMotte brings his unique talents, keen eye, and sense of humor to his writing – both fiction and non-fiction.

Retired now from the motion picture industry, Richard is devoting his time to his love of stories – writing adventures for you...

Thank You

Thank you for reading The Treasure!
If you enjoyed it, would you please leave a review on Amazon?
I would appreciate it!

Richard

www.ingramcontent.com/pod-product-compliance
Lightning Source LLC
Chambersburg PA
CBHW060324260626
47160CB00007B/2675